A
Harlequin
Romance

OTHER
Harlequin Romances
by LILIAN PEAKE

GONE
BEFORE MORNING

by

LILIAN PEAKE

HARLEQUIN BOOKS   TORONTO
WINNIPEG

Original hard cover edition published in 1973
by Mills & Boon Limited, 17 - 19 Foley Street,
London, W1A 1DR, England

SBN 373-01700-6

Harlequin edition published July 1973

Printed in Canada

CHAPTER I

WHEN Kim told her family that she was applying for a job as a housekeeper, they laughed. They were sitting round the table having their evening meal. It was the first of April and it was hailing outside.

"I should have known better than to tell them today of all days," Kim reproached herself, looking out at the weather and regarding the particles of ice that were hurling themselves savagely against the window panes as one of Nature's little jokes.

"It *is* after twelve o'clock," her brother reminded her, with a smirk.

"I am not April fooling. It's a fact."

"But, Kim," her father protested, his artistic-looking beard moving agitatedly as he spoke, "for heaven's sake, why?"

His daughter looked at him with as much joy as she had looked at the weather. When he had decided to grow his preposterous beard, she had remonstrated with him. "Whoever heard of a scientist with a beard?" she had asked. "An artist, yes. But not you, an academic to the core!"

"Why?" she echoed, and shrugged. "Why not? What else is there for me to do?"

"But, darling," her mother protested, "after all that training at university, after all your studies –"

"A lot of good they did me!" her daughter complained. "Three years of undiluted English literature, and all I managed to get was a miserable 'pass' degree. Not even second class honours."

"But surely," her brother put in, "with your training there must be better things for you to do than housekeeping?"

"What do you suggest?" Kim asked, with sisterly sarcasm. "Ticket-collector? Dustman? Window-cleaner?"

Her father leaned forward and moved his empty plate to

one side as if it were obstructing his efforts to persuade his daughter to see reason. "Housekeeping's a bit of a comedown for someone with a degree, dear. Better to be a secretary –"

"I agree with your father," her mother said. "You've had a year's training in secretarial studies –"

"Let's be honest," Kim pointed out, "I only did that to keep myself occupied while waiting for 'the' job to come along. Look," she counted on her fingers, "I've tried the Civil Service. No go. Too many applicants with better qualifications chasing too few jobs. I've tried breaking into journalism – with the same result. Advertising agencies, public relations, publishing houses – you mention it, I've tried it. Wrong sort of qualifications and too many people after the same sort of thing."

"There's always teaching," her mother said, being a teacher herself.

Kim shook her head decisively. "I haven't the burning desire to impart knowledge to others that you three seem to have." She said, a little plaintively, "I've always been the odd one out."

Her brother leaned across and patted the top of her head. "Poor lickle kiddy," he murmured in baby-talk, and his sister tried unsuccessfully to stamp on his foot under the table.

"One day, I'll write a book," she went on in the same mournful tone, "on being the only literary member of a purely scientific family."

Her father looked round expectantly for the second course which seemed to him to be an inordinately long time in coming. He gave up his search to say, "But you can't complain, my dear, that you didn't have any encouragement. In fact, your mother and I did our best to persuade you to take scientific subjects in your exams. But perversely and, knowing you, I wouldn't be at all surprised on purpose, you chose to go your own way and be different from the rest of us."

"English literature!" her brother commented, making a face. "Of all the useless subjects to specialise in. And then only to get a pass –" He shook his head and looked at her disparagingly. "After that, the only thing you can decently do, in my opinion, is get married." He said it as if it were the most unattractive job of all, and almost as useless in career prospects as English literature.

"That's a good idea," her mother said thoughtfully, "you could get married. What about Neville? You get on well with him, and Joan would make a good mother-in-law."

"There's Keith, a lecturer in the computer section at the university," her father named his place of work, "he's single and not all that bad-looking."

Her brother added, "And delighted, I'm sure, to oblige by marrying the daughter of the prof., the eminent Dr. Aldous Paton. Look at the promotion prospects within his grasp if he attached himself to the family!" He grinned at his sister's sour face. "There's also John, Ron, Don –" He stared. "Did you realise that all your boy-friends' names rhyme?"

He ducked as his sister hit out. "Anyway," Kim said, "I've got an interview at the employment agency tomorrow."

"So you're committed that far?" Her mother's voice was anxious. "Housekeeping to whom? A man?" Kim nodded. "But, darling, how do you know he's to be trusted?"

"Come off it, Mother," her son exclaimed, "this is the latter half of the twentieth century. No one talks about a 'trustworthy' man these days, where women are concerned."

Kim gave her brother a scathing look. "Speak for yourself, Perry. We all know what your morals are like. I've spoken to some of your girl-friends who visit your flat."

Her brother looked annoyed. "Have you? Which ones? I'll have to give them a stern warning not to tell tales."

Kim turned disgustedly from her brother to her mother. "I read the advertisement in a very respectable women's magazine while I was at the dentist's the other day. 'Widower with young daughter,' it said, 'requires housekeeper-gardener-cook. Must like children.' "

"Doesn't want much, does he?" Perry commented. "What's the salary?" He spoke mincingly. "Commensurate with the responsibilities?"

"I don't know," replied Kim, "and what's more, I don't much care."

"You can't take a job that isn't properly paid, Kim," her father protested, giving up waiting to be served with the rest of his meal and wandering into the kitchen to find it. His wife immediately sprang up and told him to sit down. "Apple pie, darling. I'll get it. Kim made it."

Perry made a noise of brotherly disapprobation.

"But that's one thing Kim can do," her father commented. "She can cook."

Perry looked at his sister thoughtfully. "Maybe she's right to contemplate housekeeping, even if it is only as a fill-in. You never know," he paused, "widower, did you say? He might even marry you himself!"

"Don't be silly, Perry!" His mother's voice was sharp. "We don't want Kim marrying a man old enough to be her father."

"But," Kim told her, "he can't be that old. The advertisement said, 'young daughter, must like children.' "

"There you are then," her brother grunted, tucking into his apple pie, "there's the answer to your problem. Marriage to your boss. What's his job?"

"I don't know. I'll have to ask at the interview, won't I?"

Kim kept her word and next day asked the lady interviewer the nature of the advertiser's occupation. Seconds later, she wished with all her heart that she had not done so.

"Let me see," the woman said, flicking through some documents, "Mr. Owen Lang. Er – he's a scientist, a research chemist. Responsible position, head of a large division in an internationally-known chemical firm. Financially, very stable."

Kim lowered her head to her hand. Another scientist! It could not be true. It had to be a joke, a bad dream, a nightmare. Of all things – a research chemist, like her father and her brother! And her mother, too – a teacher of chemistry in a large comprehensive school.

The interviewer, looking worried, asked, "Is there something wrong, Miss Paton?"

With difficulty, Kim recovered herself. "No, nothing wrong. Am I permitted to ask Mr. Lang's age?"

"His age?" The woman hesitated. "Well, I suppose there's

no objection to that, although as I see it, it's not really relevant. He's – er – quite young. Er – thirty-six. His wife died, let me see, five years ago."

Kim grew a little warm under the high neck of her sweater. "He's, well – just a little younger than I anticipated."

The interviewer looked at her closely and her concern changed into something very like suspicion. "I've been instructed by Mr. Lang to inform every woman who applies for this post, regardless of age, type, colouring, background, looks or shape – his words – that he has no plans whatsoever for re-marriage. He's absolutely adamant about it, and wishes me to emphasise the fact in no uncertain terms." She read from a letter on the file. "He says, 'The position being advertised is for a housekeeper only, and not a potential marriage partner. I do not wish to be regarded by any female, designing or otherwise, as "fair game" in that respect. In fact, to be frank, and in the closest confidence – oh," she stopped, "perhaps I'd better not go on."

"Please," Kim implored, "please go on. It would at least help to clarify the whole position."

The woman shrugged. "In the closest confidence, the more unattractive, shapeless and sexless the applicant is, the better I shall like it." The woman eyed her uncertainly. "My dear, not only are you much too young for this post. I hardly think you qualify on those grounds."

"But," Kim protested, "I can't help my looks, can I? And, to be as frank with you as you were with me, I desperately need this job. You see, I've been looking for one for well over a year. I'm completely unemployed, I have no money coming in, I'm a burden to my father ...' The moisture in her eyes and the pitiful tale she was putting over – which would have made her brother shake with laughter – was enough to move a slagheap, let alone an understanding, sympathetic middle-aged lady.

"All right, my dear, I'll see what I can do. You have references?"

Kim nodded, hoping her slight hesitation would pass undetected.

"You have had experience in this sort of work?" Kim nodded again, crossing her fingers under her handbag. Well, she had, hadn't she, at home while her mother was out?

"In that case," the woman went on, "there would seem to be very little against you except – er –" she eyed her rather sadly, "your elegant appearance. However, I do know that for some reason Mr. Lang is having trouble keeping his housekeepers. It seems he's rather a difficult man, so I shall put your application before him, and trust that he'll be satisfied with it."

"There is just one thing," Kim said, hoping the question she was about to ask would not ruin the image she had created of being an impoverished member of the unemployed, "if I were to be accepted for this post, would I –" she looked at the woman and decided to risk it, "would I be allowed to take my car?"

"Oh." The woman tapped on the desk top with her pencil. To Kim's relief, it seemed she had attached no significance to the fact that such a poverty-stricken young woman owned a car. "That's a question I can't answer without consultation with the prospective employer. But," she looked up encouragingly, "I could phone him and get his reaction. I have his number at work. Yes, here it is."

She dialled and waited. "Very pleasant part of the country where he lives," she said to Kim, "and near enough to your home for you to visit it occasionally. Hallo," into the mouthpiece, "may I speak to Mr. Owen Lang, please?"

There was a pause, then, "Mr. Lang's secretary? Is it possible to speak to Mr. Lang himself, please? I have a personal matter to discuss with him."

"Hallo, Lang here," came across loud and clear.

"Oh, Mr. Lang, I have y –" she pulled herself up and grimaced at Kim, "I have a lady here who is applying for the post of your housekeeper. How old?" She raised her eyebrows at Kim.

"Er – er – twenty-nine," Kim stammered, adding six years to her real age.

The woman looked sceptical but repeated over the phone

the age Kim had given her. In answer to the series of questions which the man shot at her, she gave replies which seemed to satisfy him. Then she asked about the car. There seemed to be a long pause. "Oh," the woman murmured, "I see."

She covered the mouthpiece. "He says he's never been asked such a question before." Then to the man, "Yes, she's here." She handed over the phone. "He wishes to speak to you."

Kim said, her heart pounding, "Kim Paton here." She spoke with a diffidence which was foreign to her. Timidity was not usually one of her characteristics. But the man at the other end was not to know this.

There was a long silence, interspaced with deep, regular breathing. Then, sharply, "*How* old are you supposed to be? Twenty-*nine*?"

"Y-yes, Mr. Lang." She took a grip on herself. This nervousness was getting her nowhere. If she was going to be a housekeeper then she had better sound like one. But he was speaking again.

"Twenty-nine or not, from the sound of your voice," the man said dismissively, "I simply cannot conceive of your being suitable for the post. You're not at all the kind of woman I had in mind. Add another ten or twenty years, and I might have considered it, but –"

This was more than enough to arouse her from her stupor and bring out her fighting spirit. She said frigidly, "Mr. Lang, instead of relying on instant diagnosis, like a bad doctor and, what's worse, doing so via the telephone at a distance of some forty or more miles, may I suggest that a personal interview would be more to the point? Instead of relying on the judgment of an intermediary to make up your mind for you, might I suggest that you at least give me a trial?"

She put her hand over her ear to shut out the horrified gasps of the woman at the desk, and listened instead to the prolonged and heavy silence which shouted at her from the other end of the line.

As she waited for the man's reaction to erupt in her ear, it came to her that if she were going to maintain the image of the semi-educated simpleton he visualised as being qualified to act as his housekeeper, she had better restrict the words she used to one syllable, and keep her temper under control.

But, image or no image, she was not going to be battered into submission by an unmannerly, supercilious brute of a man.

"I understand," she said into the silence, "that you're having difficulty in retaining the services of your housekeepers. I'm beginning to understand why. As far as I'm concerned, Mr. Lang, the deal, if it ever was on, is off!"

She slammed down the receiver, her face flushed with angry triumph, but paling quickly to a pinkish shade of white as she realised she had just talked herself out of the job she wanted and needed.

"I warned you, Miss Paton," the woman said, "he's a difficult man." She smiled weakly. "Not that you gave him much chance to talk! It – er – depends on how much you want a job as to whether you take this on, although," sadly, "you do seem to have queered your own pitch somewhat, don't you? So that's that, I'm afraid."

The phone rang. "Yes," the woman said, "she's still here." She listened, then covered the mouthpiece again. "He says he's so desperate for a housekeeper he's even willing to take you on. Believe me, Miss Paton, that, coming from him after the way you spoke to him, is a major, if not unheard-of concession."

She listened again and laughed slightly. To Kim she said, "He says that if you dislike him as much as you seem to before you have even met him, then he considers himself quite, *quite* safe from the possibility of your ever pursuing him for his marriage potential!" She smiled, and there was appeal in it now. "What do you say, Miss Paton? Confidentially, I've had so much trouble getting this man suited, I feel almost like bribing you to take the job!"

Kim had the odd feeling she had won the first battle in what promised to be the beginnings of a major war.

"Before I decide finally, would you please ask him again about my car?"

The woman did as Kim asked. "He says, Miss Paton, that you can bring your car if you like, but there's no question of your keeping it in the garage."

"What about the sideway?"

The woman passed the question on. "He says that's out, too. If your car were parked there, it would obstruct his free access to his own garage. It would have to be kept in the street all the time. And you would have to provide your own parking light."

Kim bristled and the woman saw it. "Miss Paton, I don't really think that's being unreasonable. If you want the job –"

Kim conceded the point. "Yes, I do want the job. I'll take it."

This piece of information was passed on to Owen Lang. "He says it will be for a trial period of three months – if you last that long."

Kim said, her voice loud with anger, "Tell that man that if I take one look at his face and don't like it, believe me, he'll be without a housekeeper before he even gets one. I'll drive straight home again."

"Miss Paton," the woman cautioned, "he'll be paying your salary, so it's for him to call the tune, don't you think?"

Kim relented and apologised. "When do I start?"

The answer came promptly. "As far as he's concerned, the sooner you take up residence and assume your responsibilities the better he will like it. When shall I say – tomorrow?"

Kim considered the position. "No. The day after." Let him wait, she thought. It will do him good.

Kim fretted away the rest of the day until her family came home.

As soon as they arrived she told them, "I've got it, I've got the job!"

She might just as well have told them the English alphabet had twenty-six letters for all the effect her statement had on them.

"Ridiculous," her father said mildly, setting the table with the air of one who is thinking "if I don't do it, no one else will!"

"That's nice," her mother said, her mind on the sausages

13

she was grilling. "At least it will fill in the time while you get a proper job."

"Implying, you'll notice," Perry smirked behind his mother's back, "that the job you've just got yourself is 'improper'! And that," he said over his shoulder, retreating out a range of his sister's feet, "wouldn't surprise me at all, from the sound of it!"

Her mother asked, when would she be starting?

"The day after tomorrow. He wanted me to start straight away, but –"

"You're keeping him waiting," her brother interrupted. "Good idea. Start as you mean to go on. Keep him dangling, like you do all the men in your life."

"So," Kim said, turning superciliously from her brother's grin, "I'll spend tomorrow packing. By the way, Mum, the woman asked about references. What shall I do? I told her I had some, but –"

"Well, dear, the domestic science teacher at school is also a part-time lecturer at the technical college where you took your secretarial course. She might be willing –"

"But, Vita," her husband called through the serving hatch, "surely it would be a blatant lie if she claimed to know all about Kim's abilities as a housekeeper?"

"Blatant fraud, I'd call it," Perry intervened. "She'd be perjuring herself."

"No, she wouldn't, Perry," his mother said mildly. "All she needs to say is that Kim was an exemplary student with an excellent character and so on, all of which is true. She was a student there, after all, even if the course she took was secretarial and not in domestic science."

"It's unbelievable," wafted through the serving hatch, "the downright deviousness of women's minds! Can't think how I ever brought myself to marry one!" But Aldous Paton came into the kitchen and kissed his wife to prove to her how glad he was that he had.

Perry asked, "What's this man's job?"

"He," said Kim through her teeth, "is a scientist, a research chemist just like you. And Dad. Not forgetting Mum."

Perry roared with laughter, and even their parents were amused. "The irony of it!" Perry croaked. "The odd one out at home, she calls herself, the only 'cultured' one in the family, as she likes to put it, and she's going to work for a 'moron' of a scientist. So she'll be the odd one out at work, too! I really must tell that one to the boys."

The night before she left, Kim packed her cases. Her mother helped her.

She said, a little sheepishly, "I told the agency woman I was twenty-nine."

"Kim, you didn't!"

"I had to, otherwise she would have said I was too young for the job."

"But, darling, you don't look twenty-three, let alone twenty-nine." Her mother studied her, hands on hips, an instant conspirator on her daughter's side. "Now, what can we do to make you look older?"

Kim swept her hair back and twisted it into a prim-looking bun at the nape of her neck. "How's that?"

"Well," her mother put her head on one side, "one can hardly say it enhances your looks. But it's a start."

"If only I wore specs. They really would make me look frightful."

"Darling, nothing would make you look frightful, with your pink and white complexion and that glorious jet black hair. But I've got just the thing – a pair of spectacles with plainglass lenses I wore in a play years ago when your father and I were interested in amateur dramatics." She went off to find them. "Here they are."

Kim put them on. "They're a bit loose."

"That's marvellous, darling. They make you look at least thirty. Now if I've got a baggy dress to lend you . . ."

The dress she found was deep purple with a prim, white-pointed collar, calf-length hem, long-sleeved and years out of date. On Kim it completed the illusion of age and dowdiness.

"This should do the trick," Kim said with satisfaction. "If I arrive on his doorstep looking like this, he'll think I'm the sort of person who won't let a man within a mile of me, let alone consider marrying one!"

Her mother laughed. "Well, if you can keep that image going, your job should be safe – and you, too! But if you once let the image slip, with your prettiness and your lovely figure, before you know where you are you'll be out of his front door with your suitcase in your hand!"

Next morning Kim said a tearful farewell to her parents. "Look after yourself," her mother called as she got into her car, "and if you have any problems, just dial our number, darling, and I'll be there at the other end to help you."

Kim waved and smiled and as she drove away, her brother's words as he had left the previous evening came back to her. "Take care – and beware," he said, laughing. "You can't trust a scientist. Take me for example!"

Although she knew he had been joking, she thought ruefully that her mother's advice was something she might well be needing before many days had passed.

CHAPTER II

THE journey to Owen Lang's house took twice as long as Kim had estimated. At first, she drove fast. The foot controlling the accelerator seemed to have become possessed of a mind of its own. Kim had physically to restrain it from pressing down to the floorboards. The rest of her responded with a kind of delirious, mindless joy. She sang to herself, "I've got a job, I've got a job." The car seemed to catch on to her buoyant mood and fling itself forward with abandoned delight.

But as she reached the half-way mark and paused for refreshment at a café adjoining a service station, her euphoria passed as if it had never been, and the bitter taste of the badly made coffee restored her balance of mind.

She started to think. What, she asked herself, clearly and dispassionately had she undertaken to do — become a house-keeper to a "difficult" and, from the sound of it, short-tempered, irascible creature with a child at a difficult, demanding age? Act as his gardener, when she hardly knew how to grow a bed of weeds, let alone cultivate plants and shrubs? And he wanted a cook. Well, that was something she could do. And she was fond of children, wasn't she — *nice* children? But the "young daughter" referred to in the advertisement might be a little fiend, having had no mother to cherish and check her for five years. So the problem remained. Like an indecisive cat on a fence, which way should she jump? On one side was a snarling animal waiting to devour her — her new employer. On the other was sanctuary — the way back home.

She struggled through the cup of brown liquid the café proprietor had misnamed coffee and crunched the plate of stale-tasting biscuits. She heard the low-toned talk of the long-distance lorry drivers around her, heard the high-pitched laughter of the girls behind the counter and envied them the straightforwardness of their lives. Money clattered into a juke

17

box and the harshness of the canned music drowned every other noise and its relentless beat forced her towards a final decision.

What should she do – turn round and go back, or carry on and meet the challenge? She stared at her car, waiting in the forecourt as if impatient to be on its way. She would not disappoint it. She scraped back her chair and stood up. Challenge it would be.

She drove on, groping for her courage like a fallen climber reaching out for a rope that had been lowered to pull him to safety from the rocks below. But her right foot had lost its impetus, its crazy desire for speed. It behaved decorously and abided by the speed limit for the remainder of the journey. Which is why it took her twice as long to reach Owen Lang's house as she had estimated.

She found the place with little trouble. It proved to be an impressive residence – too large to be called a house – standing well back from the road. Its white walls were broken into sections by imitation Tudor beams. The roof was red and deeply sloping. Kim calculated that the house must be at least sixty years old.

She took her cases from the car and carried them to the front door. She put them down and, ignoring the bell, lifted and dropped the heavy black iron knocker which, she noticed with an oddly primitive apprehension, had the shape of a ferocious-looking gargoyle. A facsimile in miniature, she wondered fearfully, of the master of the house? An omen, perhaps, of things to come?

She wondered if her new employer was at home. But it was the cleaning lady who opened the door. Her name, it seemed, was Mrs. Harker. She appeared to have been expecting Kim. All the same, she stared.

"You're not the new housekeeper, dear?"

Kim nodded, wishing she had powdered her hair with talc as her mother had suggested, to make it look grey. She stepped on to the front door mat and slid ungracefully a few inches along the hall.

"Sorry, dear," Mrs. Harker apologised, "must have polished under the mat by mistake."

Kim inhaled the lavender perfume of the polish which must have been lavishly applied. "I can smell how busy you've been."

This comment put her at once on the right side of the cleaning lady, who said she must be dying for a cup of tea, wasn't she?

"Well," said Kim, "yes, please."

The cup of tea was duly made and placed in front of her. Mrs. Harker told Kim that Mr. Lang had said there was food in the fridge and she was to help herself to whatever she could find. Kim eyed the refrigerator hungrily, but Mrs. Harker had other ideas.

"Don't have it yet, will you, till I've finished the cleaning. And whatever you do, don't make crumbs. He can't bear crumbs, that man."

Mrs. Harker washed the cups and scrubbed the sink. "He can't bear noise when he's working. He can't bear me to touch his papers. He can't bear people fussing round him. And more than anything, dear, he can't bear women!" She scrubbed the draining board. "That's why I only come once a week. It's about as much as I can stand of him. Not that I see much of him. He's usually at work, thank goodness."

"I begin to see," Kim said slowly, "why he's had a succession of housekeepers."

"You wait," Mrs. Harker said darkly, "till he gets going on you." She looked Kim up and down, noting the shapeless dress, its length, the lace-up shoes on Kim's feet. "You won't last long, dearie, if you don't mind me saying so. He'll have you with your head in your hands crying your heart out before this day's through. You've got to be tough to stand up to him."

Kim's heart plunged over the edge and crashed down on to the rocks below. And this time there was no rope of courage hanging down to haul it up again.

"Is he that bad?"

"Terrible, dear. Sorry to frighten you, but –" She pursed her lips and shook her head.

19

"Where's the little girl?"

"Next door neighbour's got her. They're youngish, got no kids. Couldn't manage it," she said cheerfully, ready with the slightest encouragement, Kim was sure, to reveal the neighbour's most personal secrets. "Funny," Mrs. Harker went on, "but they seem to get on with *him* all right. They're so good to him and his little girl, I suppose he has to be nice back. He can be, when he likes. Trouble is, dear, he doesn't often like!" And she threw back her head and shrieked with laughter.

Kim smiled weakly, glad that the woman was talkative. It saved her the bother of having to make conversation herself. And at that moment, she wanted very much to think. Again she asked herself the question – what should she do – stay, or leave at once?

Mrs. Harker was cleaning the cupboard doors and wiping over the working surfaces. "I'll tell you straight out, in case you've got ideas, he won't marry again. Had enough the first time, he said."

"What happened to his wife?" Kim's voice came out thin and brittle.

"She was an actress. And," with a smirk, "you know what actresses are. She met him at a party and hooked him there and then. He married her, being a gentleman, as he said – he told the neighbours he'd never be a 'gentleman' again with a woman. She couldn't settle down, even after the baby came. Went off gallivanting abroad on some acting tour. Plane crash. That was that."

She opened a casement window and shook out the duster. "No, he won't try it a second time. I'll tell you something he said. Got it from the neighbour." She closed the window and dusted the same surfaces again. "He says there's two types of women – and he can't abide either of 'em!" She chuckled. "The pretty ones who haven't got an intelligent thought in their heads, and the plain ones who are too brainy for words! Somehow, he says, you never get them the right way round. He said," Mrs. Harker looked at her as if trying to assess how far she could go with the newcomer, "He said the pretty ones are all right for – well, you know what, and that's all. The plain ones, they might be clever, but he wouldn't never want to sit opposite them in an armchair, let alone share a bed with 'em!" She shrieked with laughter again, sobered and peered at Kim. "Have I shocked you, dear, you not being married?"

Kim laughed in what she hoped was a knowing, careless fashion, and the woman seemed reassured.

"So don't go falling for him, dearie, although he's a good-looker and tall, too. It wouldn't be any use, no use at all."

At last she went home. Kim found the silence as unnerving as the woman's revealing chatter. She looked round the kitchen, admiring the modern fitments. Food mixer, refrigerator, deep-freeze, dishwasher, washing machine. What else could a housekeeper want? The quality of the kitchen furniture was good, the cupboards numerous, the view of the garden from the windows attractive.

She wandered round the house, trying to find her room. She wished she had remembered to stop Mrs. Harker's flow of words for a few moments and ask her.

The house was even larger than it had looked from the outside. There seemed to be a part of it which could be shut off from the rest by a door across the long narrow landing. Through the door which was standing open she found a room which she assumed to be hers.

It was large, decorated in white and pale yellow. There were built-in cupboards with sliding doors, bookshelves, a comfortable armchair with yellow velvet cushions. A white table stood in the window and a white-painted chair was pushed under it. As far as comfort was concerned, she could hardly ask for more.

The "family" section of the house consisted of a child's bedroom – no doubt the little girl's – a number of other bedrooms, and one which was larger than all the others. This, she decided, must be her employer's room. It had been tidied into impeccable neatness by Mrs. Harker's fussy hands. The double bed was covered with a lavish quilt and eiderdown, there were modern furnishings, a thick carpet, attractive curtains, but at the same time there was an unmistakably masculine air about the whole room.

21

She returned to the kitchen and looked in the fridge. She found cold meat, salad stuff and trifle. This looked like the neighbour's handiwork and she told herself she must remember to thank her for her thoughtfulness.

Hungry now, Kim ate some lunch and washed up, finding it strange to be working at another's sink. The apron which she tied round her waist, pulled the bagginess of her mother's dress into a bulging fullness above and below it.

She put on her mother's spectacles and glanced in the mirror on the kitchen wall, but turned away almost at once. She looked so dowdy she could hardly bear it. It was as if she were dressed for a part in a play. All the same, she would have to learn to tolerate her appearance. Such an image would at least keep her the job.

Her employer might not want "even to sit opposite her in an armchair" as Mrs. Harker had said, but he would surely know that such an unattractive young woman could not possibly have him – or any other man – marked down in her mind as a future husband.

There was a tap on the back door and the handle turned. "May I come in?" A woman in her late thirties stepped inside holding by the hand a pretty, fair-haired little girl whose guarded, suspicious eyes lifted to Kim's face, then fell away to stare at the floor as if it were the only friend she had in the world.

The woman, her rounded figure and warm smile offering reassurance on sight, seemed equally cautious. But after an initial start of surprise, her voice, when she spoke, was so pleasant, Kim knew at once that here was a friend.

"Welcome to the Lang ménage," the woman said. She laughed. "I nearly said menagerie, which might have been more appropriate. Owen behaves like a caged animal sometimes. I'm Daphne South and I live next door. You're Kim Paton?" Kim nodded and they shook hands. "This," said Daphne, nodding at the child, "is Candida Lang. Candy for short. She's at home today because the schools are still on holiday."

Kim held out her hand. "Hallo, Candy."

The child's hand clung to Daphne's and did not even begin to make contact with Kim's. Kim frowned. "Oh, dear," she smiled at the neighbour. "Not a very good start."

"Not to worry," said Daphne. "She'll come round. Won't you, Candy?"

"No," said Candy.

Daphne shot a swift reassuring smile at Kim. "Candy," she said, releasing the child's hand, "go and play in the garden, dear."

Glad to escape, Candy went without protest.

"The point is," Daphne explained, sitting down, "she's had to shake hands with so many housekeepers in the last few months, and my dear, they've come – and gone – in so many odd shapes and sizes –" she eyed Kim's dress a little uncomfortably, "the poor child's given up hope, I think. She told me this morning that she hated you even before she saw you. She knew you'd be 'awful', as she put it, just like all the others."

Kim flopped into a chair. "Oh dear," she repeated, "there seems to be so much against me."

"Not to worry," Daphne soothed again, "if you ever feel you can't stand it, just come and let off steam to me. All the others did, so I'm used to it!" She rose to go. "Found your bedroom yet?"

Kim described the room she thought was hers and Daphne confirmed it.

"He gave me three months," Kim said, "three months' trial."

Daphne hooted with laughter. "Three *months*, did you say? Wishful thinking on his part, my dear. Some of the others lasted less than three *weeks*!" She went to the door. "I'll leave you to it. Remember, if you ever feel like screaming, just pop into my house."

As she went out, Kim remembered to thank her for the food. Daphne acknowledged her thanks with a careless wave of the hand.

Candy stayed in the garden for some time. When she did come in she raced through the kitchen and up the stairs as though a crowd of rioters was at her heels.

"This," Kim told herself grimly, "is not going to be easy."

To take her mind off her troubles, she started planning the evening meal. She found a packet of frozen pastry in the freezer and set it aside to thaw. She would make a cheese and onion flan and follow it with a baked sponge pudding and custard.

The flan was one of the best she had ever made, and the pudding was golden brown and firm to the touch. "Now for the custard," she said to herself. As she stirred the thickening yellow liquid, the steam rising from it clouded the lenses of her glasses. She removed them impatiently and continued stirring the custard for a moment or two longer.

She was in the act of lifting the saucepan from the cooker when a noise behind her made her start so violently that some of the custard erupted from the saucepan and gushed like yellow lava to the floor.

A man filled the doorway, hands in pockets, eyes glinting like sun on ice, his expression sardonic and deriding. He was tall, his dark hair was brushed back from his temples, his shoulders were broad with a suggestion of belligerence about them but which could undoubtedly offer refuge and comfort to anyone who had the temerity to seek them there. His mouth, though well-shaped, had a tautness about it which disclosed an innate cynicism and a ruthless nature, unsparing to his enemies and to anyone who dared to incur his displeasure.

"You, no doubt, are Miss Kim Paton."

It was a statement rather than a question. A nod was all Kim could manage.

"Which means that you're the latest in my long line of temporary housekeepers."

"That's quite right, Mr. Lang," she gushed in an over-eager voice, yet hating herself for being so ingratiating. She realised she was still holding the saucepan of custard, so she returned it to the cooker, searched for her glasses and pushed them on as though she was as helpless as a babe without them. Holding out her hand in a welcoming gesture, she walked towards him.

"How do you do, Mr. Lang?"

But he plainly regarded her stay in his home as being of such short duration that it must have seemed to him that her hand was not worth the shaking. He looked at it as though it was as irrelevant as a fur coat in midsummer and kept his own hand to himself. Thrown off balance, Kim rubbed hers against the side of her apron as if the palm had somehow become coated with dirt.

So her hand remained untouched by yet another member of that family. Obviously – her sense of humour struggled to the aid of her ruffled pride – an aversion to handshaking was an inherited trait! She felt convinced that if there had been a pet attached to the household it, too, would have deliberately withheld its paw had she had the audacity to try and shake it!

Now he was looking with undisguised distaste at the shapeless bundle in front of him. He plainly detested the old-fashioned hair-style and the dark-brown horn-rimmed spectacles which sat so insecurely on the bridge of her nose. She raised her right forefinger and pushed them back into place.

"I'm cooking your evening meal, Mr. Lang," she volunteered over-brightly, as if that alone would convince him of her efficiency as a housekeeper.

"Miss Paton," he folded his arms and leaned against the door frame, "even if I were a half-witted idiot, I could see that." Her desire to please him began to recede like the sea at the turn of the tide. "I also have a highly-developed sense of smell, and judging by the foul odour with which this kitchen is suffused at this moment, your efforts have been in vain. I cannot stand onions, neither the taste nor the smell." He lifted himself to his full height. "However, my daughter is not averse to them, unfortunately, so she will no doubt agree to sample your cooking, if you ask her nicely." He closed the door and went away.

It was then that she began to hate him. She opened the oven door and looked at her flan, her perfect flan, the dish for which even her own family praised her and which had been dismissed so contemptuously without trial by her new employer.

But, she reasoned, if she wanted to keep the job – and there was no doubt that she did – she would have to get to know his likes and dislikes, and learn to cultivate the servility which, judging by his supercilious manner, he seemed to demand from his housekeepers.

The dining-room was empty and she set the table, opening the sideboard drawers and cupboards and discovering in them everything she needed. Returning to the kitchen, she looked in the refrigerator. There were two slices of cold meat left over from her lunch. That, with a tomato, would have to suffice for Owen Lang's evening meal. And if that did not please him, he would just have to go hungry.

Ten minutes later, he reappeared at the kitchen door. "Isn't it time I was given something to eat?"

Her back was to him, so he did not see the fire in her eyes, but she took her temper by the scruff of the neck and shook it into submission. Then, with remarkable self-control, she turned and smiled at him, apologetically.

"I'm sorry it's taking me so long, Mr. Lang, but it is my first day here and one is bound to make mistakes ..." Her voice tailed off on a note of appeal.

"If you are as capable and efficient at your job as that reference I received about you led me to believe, then you should have made all your mistakes in the past. I did not take you on as an apprentice, but as a fully qualified, fully competent housekeeper." He slammed the door behind him.

She ground her teeth, her temper nearly shaking free of her clutching hold. She carried in his food on a tray and placed it before him.

"I'm sorry," she apologised yet again, her tone as submissive as she could make it, "for having cooked something you dislike. I do hope this cold meat will suit you. I'm afraid it's all I could find at such short notice."

"Oh, put it down," he snapped. "I'll have to make do with it, won't I?" He picked up his knife and fork. "What, for heaven's sake, have you conjured up for second course?"

"Baked pudding, Mr. Lang." Her smile held mute appeal. "Will that suit you?"

26

He glowered. "How can I tell until I've tried it?"

She took a deep breath. "Yes, Mr. Lang," she said, forcing a rueful smile, "of course you can't. How silly of me!"

He put down his knife and fork, folded his arms and turned his eyes contemptuously on her flushed face. "Miss Paton, as I told all my other housekeepers, if there's one thing I cannot stand above all others, it's a simpering, servile woman. I find your fawning submissiveness nauseating."

The breath she took was a gasp, but she strangled her retort at birth. "Mr. Lang," she said hoarsely, "shall I call your daughter down to join you?"

He resumed his eating. "Are you giving her that abomination you tried to serve to me?"

"My cheese and onion flan, Mr. Lang? Yes, Mr. Lang."

"Then she will not join me. She'll have her meal with you. I told you, I can't stand the smell of onions."

"Then," she said, with a grim sarcastic smile, "I shall have to serve them more often, won't I, Mr. Lang?" Her heart shot out fountains of joy as she watched the astonishment spill out of his eyes. She closed the door and went upstairs in search of Candy, her spirits as light as her footsteps.

But her newfound joy did not last. She found Candy lying on her stomach on her bedroom floor, a comic spread out in front of her.

"Candy dear, your tea's ready." Kim's smile was warm in spite of the cold dislike in the child's blue eyes. Kim thought she might have to use persuasive tactics, but the little girl was too resigned for opposition. She obeyed lifelessly, complying without question even when Kim suggested that she "washed her hands, dear."

Feeling that the child was too tractable to be true, Kim told her, "You're having your tea with me, Candy, not with your daddy. Do you mind?"

Candy shrugged, hatred shouting from her eyes. Kim would rather she had kicked and screamed her hatred out. It would have been easier to handle than this cold, frightening resignation.

They ate in silence. When Kim carried the baked pudding

in to the dining-room, the man sitting in solitary state at the table received the food in silence, too. Like father, like daughter, Kim thought. They had both brought uncommunicativeness to a fine art.

When Kim returned to collect his empty plate, she asked, her voice toneless, "Would you like coffee, Mr. Lang?"

He looked at her as though she were mad. "Of course I want coffee."

She smiled, saying sweetly, "I just wondered if that was something you simply couldn't stand, like so many other things."

Something flickered across his eyes. It might have been suspicion, it might have been anger, but whatever it was sounded a note of warning inside her. Even if he did say he disliked servility, it seemed to be more acceptable to him than revolt.

"I'll bring it as soon as I've made it, Mr. Lang," she told him, reverting to her placatory tone of voice. She made the coffee and put it in front of him and he dismissed her with a nod.

As soon as Candy had finished her tea she raced out of the kitchen and up the stairs like an athlete in training for the Olympics. Kim stacked the dishes on the draining board, intending to wash them by hand. She eyed the dishwasher nervously and peered inside, wishing she had the courage to operate it.

Owen Lang came into the kitchen and emptied an ash tray into the pedal bin. "What's the matter? Don't tell me you're scared of a piece of kitchen equipment? It won't bite."

She smiled deprecatingly. "Of course not, Mr. Lang. I was –" She looked up at him uncertainly. "I was just wondering how it works."

"Don't tell me," he said again, "that this paragon, this supremely efficient housekeeping robot whose services I've temporarily acquired doesn't know how to operate a dishwasher?"

She shook her head. "In the places I've – worked, they've never had such a thing. Washing machine, yes, but washing-*up* machine, no."

She found herself wishing that her father had not been so

resolute in his refusal to buy one for her mother. "*I* do the drying up, while you wash," he would say whenever she had broached the subject. "It's something we share." And there the discussion had always ended, with her father winning. Now Kim wished he hadn't.

Owen Lang seemed slightly puzzled. "I have a freezer. I take it you know how to manage that piece of equipment?"

She turned to him eagerly. "Oh, a freezer, yes. My mother —" She stopped, just in time, but his eyes demanded an explanation. "My mother — er — often read advertisements and collected leaflets about them —" She stopped again, hoping he would be satisfied. How could she tell him they had an enormous freezer stocked to capacity in the garage at home?

"But," he took her up, "she could never afford one?"

"Well," she licked her lips, not wishing to tell an outright lie, "well, she —"

He nodded as if he understood. "I'd better explain how this thing works."

He did more, he did the entire washing up. But his tolerance of her ignorance did not last. He looked round the kitchen.

"I trust there's no other piece of equipment in here you claim to be unable to work? The tap, for instance? The pedal bin?"

The sarcasm was back and it made her bridle, but she patted her anger on the head and rocked it back to sleep.

"It was very kind of you, Mr. Lang," she said meekly, "to help me. I'm sorry I didn't know how to use the dishwasher, but I'll try not to trouble you about anything else."

He pushed his hands into his pockets and looked at her narrowly. "I can't believe it," he muttered. "Where's the vitriol gone?"

She frowned. "Vitriol, Mr. Lang?"

"Yes, the stuff you poured into my ear the other day via the employment agency's telephone. Where's the woman whose 'diagnosis' was so 'instant' — that was what you accused me of, wasn't it? — so instant that she hated the sight of me before she had even set eyes on me? That was the only reason I engaged you. Now it seems you're just like the rest. I told you earlier and I repeat it now – I can't stand a simpering woman. I suspect her motives. All the women I've had here have either been optimistic widows or – like yourself – hopeful virgins. And they have all – like yourself – tried making up to me, getting round me by being too obsequious for words and overflowing with a desire to please. All with only one object in mind – marriage, to me."

"Is that what you think I'm after, Mr. Lang?" Her voice was quiet but intense. If there was going to be a war between them, then she would make quite sure it would not be a cold war. She would show him what she was made of. She fought her battles to win them, however formidable her opponent. Words were the most effective amunition at her disposal, and the words she chose were designed to hit their target good and hard.

"Marriage – to you? Let me disillusion you completely on that score at the start of our relationship. Judging by what I've seen and heard of you from the moment I made your acquaintance, if you were the only marriageable man left on earth, I wouldn't want to marry you!"

He straightened himself and murmured, with a smile, "That's what all the others said when I challenged them. Nevertheless they all left next day, having realised that they had no chance whatsoever of achieving their objective." He took out his cheque book. "Now, do I give you a day's pay, Miss Paton? Will you be leaving in the morning?"

So her ammunition had hit the target, but he had caught her verbal bullets and used them as missiles and fired them back at her. She tried again, mixing in with her words the vitriol he seemed to expect from her.

Her tone was reasonable, but spiked. "You know, Mr. Lang, you really do beat the lot! You're the most objectionable creature – I won't denigrate the word 'man' by using it – I've ever come across. They warned me about you, all of them –"

He raised his eyebrows. "But you came nevertheless." He moved his hand with a flourish. "There you are. That proves my point. There was only one thing you were after, just like the others – marriage."

"One day," she said, her voice grating, "I'll give you a list of things I 'can't stand'. At the top of it will be conceited, arrogant, overbearing, supercilious *men*!" She turned from his gloating smile and ran up the stairs.

But her troubles were not over. She found Candy sprawled across the bed. She had been reading but had dropped the comic and was staring at the ceiling. She did not have the look of a child whose eyes were acting out an imaginary scene against the backcloth of whiteness, or tracing out the patterns made by the numerous cracks which had formed in the ceiling.

She was simply staring and when her eyes swivelled round to look at Kim, they were lifeless and without hope, like a person mourning the absence of a loved one. Kim stood beside the bed and wished she could think of something to say which would break through to the secret places in the child's mind.

But it was Candy who started the conversation. "What's your name?"

"Kim," was the answer.

"Miss Kim?"

"No, Kim Paton, but you can call me Kim."

Candy's head moved negatively from side to side against the yielding softness of the bedclothes. "Daddy wouldn't let me. I'll have to call you Miss Paton."

"But it's *my* name, Candy, and if *I* say you can use it, then you can."

The child's head moved again. "Don't want to. It would mean you were my friend, and you're not. You're just the housekeeper." She asked without interest, "Will you be leaving soon, like all the others?"

"Of *course* not!" Kim found herself gushing in an effort to convince the child. "I'm staying a long, long time."

Candy said, her voice drained of colour, "That's what all the others said. But they didn't, and I was glad. You won't stay, either."

Kims temper stirred irritably like a sleeping dog being pestered by a child. With a struggle she quietened it. Whatever happened, she must deal gently with this little girl, she must

31

restrain the urge to fight back. But she knew also that it would prove to be the most difficult task she had ever undertaken.

"Well," she said over-brightly, "if you call me Miss Paton, I'll have to call you Miss Lang, won't I?" She expected the child to smile, but she merely shrugged and picked up her comic.

Kim turned away at the child's dismissal, irritable at her own failure to communicate. She jerked up her wrist so that she could see her watch. "Shouldn't you be getting ready for bed – dear?" She forced out the endearment.

"Not till Daddy tells me."

"Do you always wait until he tells you?"

Candy nodded. "Sometimes he forgets and then he gets annoyed with me because I didn't remind him and it's so late when he remembers."

There was nothing for it, Kim decided, she would have to see the child's father and clarify the position. She went downstairs and tapped on the sitting-room door. It was empty. She looked in the dining-room. He was working at the table and papers were spread all over it.

He frowned. "What do you want?"

She smiled apologetically, holding back her irritation at his expression. "Sorry to disturb you, Mr. Lang –"

"Oh, cut out the niceties. You have disturbed me. Now get to the point."

"Your daughter," Kim said, swallowing her pride as if it were unpalatable medicine, "is waiting for you to tell her to go to bed."

He put down his pen and leaned back, arms folded. "Is she really?" He looked her over. "And what do I employ you for, if not to take decisions like that? Such momentous decisions, too."

She breathed hard, gripped the back of a chair and, because she could not lash out at the man who was addressing her so contemptuously, maltreated the wood beneath her fingers instead.

"Mr. Lang, if I had been informed at the beginning that the timing of her going to bed was to be left to me, that it was one of my duties to act as nursemaid as well as housekeeper, I would naturally have carried out such duties without question." With an agitated finger she pushed up the glasses which would keep slipping down her nose. "As a domestic servant," she used the expression deliberately, but his steady gaze resting on her face did not flicker, "I may have all the qualities attributed to me in that reference, but I have never *ever* claimed to be a mind-reader. So the next time you want me to do something, perhaps you would be so good as to *tell* me and not expect me to guess."

He smiled. "Miss Paton, it would do just a little to enhance your – looks, if you had those spectacles you wear tightened so that they fitted you. Each time they slip, I suppose you realise you're not looking through the optical centre?"

She slammed the door, counted twenty and walked slowly up the stairs.

"Candy dear," she said sweetly, "your daddy says it's time for bed."

Candy put down her comic and sat up. "He hasn't told me."

"No, dear, but he told me to tell you." Candy looked at her suspiciously. "I may be a horrid old housekeeper, but I don't tell tales, Candy."

The child's eyes opened a fraction wider, then dropped to study her bare knees as if their construction puzzled her. "Nor do I," she said. Kim waited. "Tell lies," Candy added.

Kim knew exactly what the child wanted her to say – that no "nice" little girl told lies, so being a nice little girl, of course she didn't. But Kim shrugged. "Don't you? I thought everyone told lies at certain times, like when we pretend to like someone and really we hate them."

"That's not *telling* a lie," said Candy, "that's acting one."

"Mm," Kim pretended to consider the matter. "Perhaps you're right," she said, and went out.

"Miss Kim – I mean, Miss Paton." Candy called her back and Kim had to hide her astonishment. "I – I don't want you to help me get undressed."

So this was another test. "I wouldn't dream of helping you, Candy. Big girls don't need to be helped with anything, and

33

from the look of you, you're a big girl, aren't you?"

"Yes, I am," said Candy with pride – and a smile.

Kim went into her room and flopped on to the bed. Obviously she had passed that test, too. She looked at her suitcases, standing forlornly in the centre of the room where she had dropped them on arrival. Well, should she unpack them? Or, come the morning, should she leave?

CHAPTER III

KIM removed her mother's spectacles and threw them aside. They were heavy on her nose and had left a mark which she tried to rub away without success. She would not wear them again. She removed her apron. Her mother's dress hung limply from the shoulders, bunching bulkily under the belt to emerge and sag sadly to the hem well below her knees.

The thought of her mother made her long to hear the sound of her voice. After Candy was in bed she would ask permission to use the telephone. She would speak to her parents. She would whisper so that her employer could not hear, and she would ask her mother what to do. It irked her always to give up anything she had started, even an impossible task such as this, but she doubted if she could stand it much longer. Well, she had been warned. She had taken a calculated risk and now she must decide whether or not to take the consequences.

Out of the window she could see the large attractive garden – rockeries, lawns, flower beds, apple trees, even a vegetable patch at the end. That would be her job, too, if she stayed. What was it he had asked for? Housekeeper, cook, gardener ... He had omitted the child-minder part from the advertisement, perhaps deliberately. What he wanted, she told herself sourly, was a wife – and there she caught at her thoughts like a cricketer cutting off the flight of a cricket ball. Forbidden territory. Anyway, what woman could stand him?

The garden next door where the Souths lived was in impeccable order. There was a man working out there now, even in the gathering dusk. She supposed it was Daphne's husband. Nice man, he looked, around forty, dressed in gardening clothes, digging fiercely as if the work he was doing must be finished before nightfall.

She sighed and turned away. If it were not for that horror

35

of a man sitting downstairs, she might eventually have settled down in the job and even come to like it, perhaps. She called to Candy,

"Are you ready yet?"

A small, tired voice answered, "Yes."

Kim went into the child's bedroom. She was sitting up in bed, fresh, sweet and very young in her flower-patterned pyjamas and her tangled fair hair.

"Have you washed?" Candy nodded. "Shall I just run the comb through your hair?" Candy shrank away. "Slide down," Kim said, "I'll cover you up.'

"No need," mumbled Candy, but Kim did cover her, nevertheless. The sweet pale face looked up at her, wondering, wondering ... Kim caught the expression and it tugged at her heart. She bent down and kissed the soft, smooth cheek. With deliberation, the child seized a handful of sheet and rubbed the kiss away. The eyes that looked up at Kim held resentment and rebuff. They were her father's eyes, pale blue, deadly cold and utterly unloved.

Kim closed the bedroom door, stood for a moment on the landing fighting the tears that had welled up, because of the child's rejection, because of her own misery and because of the profound pity she felt for the unhappy little girl who lay in bed on the other side of that door.

Kim had never felt so wretched. She sat, chin in one hand, pulling absently with the other at the hairpins which kept the bun in place at the nape of her neck. If she phoned her mother now they would probably be watching television, or working. But whatever they were doing she knew they would not mind being interrupted.

She did not relish disturbing her employer again, but there was no alternative.

"Now what, Miss Paton?" he asked irritably.

"Would you have any objection to my using your telephone, Mr. Lang? I should like to phone my –"

"Boy-friend?" he cut in mockingly.

She answered sharply, not caring what his reaction might

be, "If I wanted to phone my boy-friend, I should have to toss up. I have three." That should squash him, she thought, with grim satisfaction.

But his grin broadened. "Now how could someone like *you*," his gaze travelled disparagingly over her, "net *three* boy-friends? Is all that primness I see before me just a veneer, a thin coating of 'touch-me-not' which has the opposite effect and simply makes a man more eager?"

She smiled sweetly. "You should know, Mr. Lang. You're a man. I'm not."

He cleared his throat. "Neatly lobbed back into my side of the court, Miss Paton. Congratulations. I didn't know you had it in you." He looked up at her suddenly as if he were enjoying himself. "Your service."

"May I use your phone, please? I want to speak to my mother."

He looked surprised. "Is your mother on the phone?"

"Yes, of course." Then she remembered her role. "I mean, yes, it's a luxury, but my parents think it's so useful if they – er – ever need a doctor." She really would have to watch herself. "I'll pay for the call, of course."

He waved the offer aside. "Go ahead and use the phone. I'm going out to the garage, anyway."

The front door closed behind him. Relieved that she could now speak frankly to her mother without fear of being overheard, she dialled the number. "Kim here, Perry. Is Mum there?"

"Hallo," her brother said, surprised. "Something wrong? Has he raped you already? I did try to warn you, didn't I?"

"Stop fooling, Perry." At that point her mother took over. "Hallo, Mum. Listen, tell me what I should do." She fell over herself in getting the words out and her misery came tumbling from her. She told her mother about her impossible employer, his sarcastic manner, his intolerance, his downright rudeness. She told her about his little daughter who hated her and was determined to go on doing so for as long as she stayed there.

"I even tried kissing her," Kim went on, "but she wiped it off. They both expect me to leave, and I think, in their

37

hearts, they *want* me to leave. I'm told that Mr. Lang has been so horrible to all his previous housekeepers, they've almost worn a dent in the front garden path with their comings and goings. I hate it here, Mum, I don't think I can stand it."

"Darling, tell him who you are, then he might have more respect for you."

"Meaning that he might be an intellectual snob and tolerate me better if he hears about my family background?" She thought, "Tell him I've got a four-car family, a beautiful modern house to live in, with all the modern equipment he possesses, that my father is a university professor who has written textbooks, that I've got a brother with a degree, a mother with a degree and myself with a —"

"Oh, no, I couldn't do that," she told her mother, "he would say I was here under false pretences and he would be right. No, it isn't that. It's because I'm a woman."

"Because you're a *woman*? But, darling, what else did he expect you to be — neuter?"

There were roars of laughter from the other end and her brother said into the telephone, "Go all feminine on him, Kim — all clinging and womanly. With everything else you've got — and you may be my sister, but boy, have you got it! — he won't stand a chance!"

Kim had to smile. "Just to remind you, Perry, you're not talking to one of your girl-friends, only your sister."

"I know."

"Then pardon me while I faint dead away for a few moments."

"Well," said Perry, "it sounds as if you've reached rock-bottom and need someone to haul you up and give you a bit of self-confidence. Cheer up, girl! Don't let the blighter grind you down, as they say. Here's Dad."

"Kim?" her father said. "The advantages are all on your side, my dear. He's relying on you for his welfare, he's in your hands. Remember that. Here's Vita."

Her mother added a few more words of comfort and wisdom. "Just keep kissing that poor little girl, darling, like I used to do to you. That's what she needs, a little bit of love."

38

"Thanks, Mum, thanks —" her voice faltered, "Thanks for being so understanding, all of you. 'Bye."

Now there were tears in her eyes, tears of thankfulness that she had a family who rallied round her so loyally and lovingly when she needed them.

"Running home to mother, Miss Paton?" The sarcastic voice came from the kitchen door. Kim swung round. He must have come in the back way. "So soon? Am I to take it you'll be gone before morning, like all the others?"

Then he saw the tears. "Don't turn those on. I've seen them so often. Tears harden my heart, Miss Paton, they don't soften it."

She blinked away her tears and in the turmoil of emotions brought about inside her by the sudden severing of the lifeline which had connected her for a few moments to her family, her temper broke free from the restraints she had so determinedly placed on it since he had come home. It snarled and bared its teeth.

"For your information, Mr. Lang, you don't possess a heart. Instead, you've got a large chunk of rock where your heart should be. And if you think you're going to get rid of me that easily, then you're in for a shock. If it's a bit of wishful thinking on your part, who am I to stop you indulging in it? If you're saying it merely to put the idea into my head, then you're wrong again. It's been there since I first heard your voice on the telephone the other day. The only trouble, from your point of view, is that I don't intend to act upon it."

She saw the sardonic smile — was his smile never genuine and warm? — and went to the front door. "I'm going out to put the lights on my car, since I'm not allowed to park it in the sideway. Then I'm going upstairs — to *unpack*!"

She unlocked the car and switched on the sidelights, hoping the battery would not be flat by morning. She left the little car with reluctance. The upholstery felt so familiar, like the welcome face of a friend in a crowd. Its outline as it hugged the kerb looked so reassuring, she was tempted to spend the night in it, as if it were an extension of her own home.

As she entered the hall, he called her into the sitting-room.

He did not invite her to sit down. He said, "I understand that your family is suffering from some – er – financial embarrassment."

She began to shake her head but thought it prudent to await developments. "How –?" she began.

"How do I know? I phoned the employment agency the other day after you'd gone. They explained why you were so anxious to get this job. You were out of work, they said, and urgently needed the money."

"Well, I – er . . ." Good heavens, what could she say? But it explained his surprise at her parents' possession of a telephone. "I – I know it was a bit of an – embarrassment to my father to have me at home without bringing in any money, and," she rushed on, "my mother goes – *has* to go out to work." Well, it was true, wasn't it? Her mother had said so herself time and again because if she didn't, "boredom would drive her mad".

She wished he would stop looking at her so keenly. "Would it help you," he said, "to assist them financially if I increased your salary?"

She was overcome with astonishment and guilt. With his impossible nature, philanthropy was something she never dreamed he possessed. What was his motive? Was he testing her again?

"Good heavens no, Mr. Lang. I mean, I wouldn't dream of asking you –"

"You're not asking me. I'm offering."

"But I couldn't accept it, Mr. Lang –"

"Good God, here's the first woman I've ever met who's actually turning down the offer of more money!" He became cynical. "You really will have to join a trade union, Miss Paton, and learn to fight *for* your rights, instead of against them! All the same, your salary will be increased as from now." He named a sum. "That should enable you to give them more financial help."

She shook her head violently, but in vain. For the record, she told herself, if he ever discovers the truth, let it be remembered that I refused, I really refused!

She gushed over with gratitude, thinking that in doing so he would see how much she appreciated his generosity. But he waved her thanks away. "For God's sake don't go all sycophantic on me. I told you, I can't stand fawning women."

Now he had reverted to normal, his sudden benevolence overridden by his habitual cynicism. With a nervous gesture arising out of the awkward situation in which his charity had placed her, she raised her forefinger to push back non-existent spectacles. Too late she remembered she had taken them off.

He saw the movement and frowned. "Why are you not wearing them? Because they're too loose?"

"Not exactly, I —"

"It probably was, all the same, because of my remark earlier about their habit of slipping down. Go and get them. I'll tighten them for you. I know how to do it."

"No, thank you," she said hastily, "it was just —"

"Nothing annoys me more, Miss Paton," he put down his pen and stood up, pushing away his chair with the back of his legs, "than a woman who ought to wear glasses, but is too vain to do so. In any case, my motive is not entirely altruistic. If you're not wearing your glasses when you should be, your work might suffer, and after the increase in salary I've just given you," his smile became mocking, "that I simply could not tolerate. You see, I want my money's worth. Go and get them."

She shook her head. "It really doesn't matter, Mr. Lang . . ."

He made for the door. "Where are they, in your room?"

She cut him off and raced up the stairs, bringing the spectacles down, her heart thudding, knowing it was inevitable now that he would discover they were only stage props. But he did not seem to suspect any deep-laid plot to mislead him.

"Put them on," he ordered. She did so and he pushed under her mass of hair with his fingers and felt behind her ears. "They're a complete misfit. If I were you, I shouldn't patronise that particular optician again. He doesn't know his job."

"No, Mr. Lang," she said meekly, and he raised an eyebrow at her docility, his suspicions still not aroused.

41

He went into the kitchen, walked across to the electric cooker and switched on a hotplate, waiting a few seconds for the heat to increase. Then he waved each earpiece gently over the heat until the plastic had softened sufficiently to be pliable. With the same care, he bent the ends to curve more sharply.

"Now try them." She put them on and his fingers slid round the earpieces again. She had the greatest difficulty in not shrinking from his touch.

"A little more adjustment, I think, then they should fit you properly." He held the glasses to the light. "What are you, short-sighted, long-sighted, or do you suffer from astigmatism and cannot focus correctly?"

She reached up to snatch them away before he learned the truth, but she was too late.

He lowered the spectacles and looked at her, his eyes narrow. "These are plain glass. Did you know?"

"I – I –" How could she deny it? Colouring deeply, she nodded.

His eyes were deadly cold. "So why did you wear them? Would you kindly explain?"

"It was because –" How could she tell him she had put them on to make herself so unattractive to him he could not possibly suspect that she was chasing after him as he had alleged all the other women had done? "I'm sorry, I can't explain."

"Can't or won't?"

She paused. "Won't."

"I see." He handed them back to her. "No wonder you were so reluctant to let me look at them at close quarters. I can't of course force you to explain, but –" he looked her over frigidly, "I begin to wonder what else there is about you that's false."

Dear heaven, she thought, if only you knew! She said, in a small voice, "If you want to withdraw that increase in salary, Mr. Lang, I shall quite understand."

"Oh, go away," he said, motioning her to the door.

She opened it and turned. "Do you require any more food, Mr. Lang, before you go to bed? A hot drink, perhaps?"

"I have a hot drink, but I make it myself."

"Would you object, Mr. Lang, if I made myself one?"

"Oh, make yourself what the blazes you like. Only get out!"

"Yes, Mr. Lang. Goodnight, Mr. Lang. And thank you, Mr. Lang."

He sat down abruptly, grinding his teeth.

She unpacked her cases before she got into bed.

By the time Kim arrived downstairs the following morning, Owen Lang had breakfasted.

She apologised. "I'm so sorry, I forgot to ask what time you got up."

"I'm an early riser, Miss Paton."

"So I see. You should have called me, Mr. Lang."

"Yes, I should, but I thought you might need your – beauty sleep." The mocking smile belied his sincerity.

She became conscious of her mother's dress and the deadly dull hair-style. Well, at least the disguise seemed to be achieving its object. He obviously regarded her as being totally undesirable. He had not even begun to guess – and really, looking at her own reflection she was not surprised – that the dress concealed a shape which was the envy of all her friends. Which was what her brother had been talking about.

Her employer took a bunch of keys from his pocket and held them out. "Since I imagine you'll be staying until at least your first pay-day," he had agreed to give her a weekly salary, "I'll hand over this duplicate set of keys."

She thanked him. "What time will you be home this evening, Mr. Lang?"

"Six-ish. I shall require a two-course meal. Er – minus onions, if you please."

She nodded. "I've placed them second to the top of the list which I'm making of your pet hates, Mr. Lang."

He looked interested. "The top one being?"

"Women, Mr. Lang."

He gave the first genuine laugh she had heard from him. "You had me there, Miss Paton. I asked for that."

Kim sighed with relief when he had gone. She was wondering what to do about Candy when she heard her go into the bathroom. Kim ran up the stairs and asked, "Want any help, Candy dear?"

Candy did not answer. Bearing in mind her mother's advice and making her voice soft and kindly, Kim persisted, "Can you manage, Candy?"

The child opened the bathroom door. "Yes," she said, and closed it again.

Kim took a grip of herself. "Bad start number two," she thought.

Candy dragged her feet down the stairs, had a bowl of cereal, a cup of milk, then rushed out of the kitchen door. Since the morning was overcast and chilly, Kim called, "If you're going to play outside, Candy, you should put on your coat."

But Candy opened the side door, raced into the Souths' garden and disappeared into Daphne's kitchen, where she stayed for the rest of the morning.

Kim shrugged. Perhaps it was better that way, at least at first. Later, if she stayed the course, Candy could not go finding sanctuary with the neighbours every day. It would not be fair to the Souths.

She made the beds, folding her employer's blue pyjamas carefully and pushing them under his pillow. Odd, she thought, that he still slept in a double bed. She put away the suit he had left on a chair and placed his shoes on a rack which was tucked away in a corner of the room. The shirt and socks he had left on the floor she placed in the half-full linen basket.

She wandered back into her own room and wondered what to do next. The purple dress was getting her down. Since her employer was away all day, why shouldn't she wear something more comfortable and change back before he came home?

She tugged the dress over her head and pulled on a long-sleeved sweater and navy slacks, belting them tightly round the waist. She loosened her long black hair, letting it hang freely down to her shoulders. She pushed her feet into brown toeless sandals and put the lace-up shoes she had been wearing into the wardrobe.

When she looked at her reflection, she felt cheered beyond words. This was the Kim Paton she knew, not that dowdy young-old lady who had glowered back at her every time she looked in the mirror. Boldly she put colour on her lips and pencilled in her eyebrows. Better still. She went about her business with a lighter heart.

With Owen Lang out of the house, the whole atmosphere improved. The job became almost acceptable. She prepared a light lunch for herself and Candy, hoping the child would like it. She flicked a duster quickly over the furniture and went into the garden to pick some spring flowers. There were daffodils and hyacinths in full bloom and she searched for vases in the kitchen cupboards. Some of the flowers she put in the dining-room, breathing in their delicate perfume as she did so, others she carried into the sitting-room, keeping back a small bunch for the kitchen.

At lunch-time she called next door for Candy. Daphne opened the back door and said, "Hal –" and stopped in midword. She took a breath and started again. "Hal-*lo*!" She gazed wide-eyed at the girl on the doorstep. "My word, what a transformation! Like a chrysalis emerging into a butterfly. And a beauty at that. Whatever happened to that dowdy old lady I met yesterday?"

"Oh," said Kim cheerfully, "she'll come back this evening."

"But, for heaven's sake, why?" Daphne opened the kitchen door wider. "Come in and tell me all. Candy's upstairs, so you can speak freely."

Kim sat in a chair which Daphne pulled out for her. She eyed the neighbour cautiously, wishing she could tell her, longing to do so. "If I did, would you promise to keep it to yourself, every word?"

Daphne nodded vigorously. "Every single word, on my honour."

So Kim told her everything. She explained about her home background, her family, her university education and her total lack of experience in anything even remotely connected with housekeeping.

"So you're afraid Owen will think you're after him?" Daphne laughed loudly. "Looking at you as you are, my dear, I have a feeling the biter will be bit."

"Oh, he won't see me as I am. I'll change back every time he comes home."

Daphne shrugged. "Good luck to you, that's all I can say." She laughed again. "But there's something I must tell you, dear, and as far as you're concerned, it's only fractionally less off-putting than his obsessive fear of your chasing him. You know he's a scientist? He's in research, man-made fibres, actually." She eyed Kim uncomfortably. "You're not going to like this one bit, dear, but he can't, simply cannot stand arts graduates – people like you, in fact. Useless types, he calls them. And a lot more names, besides."

"Oh dear! Another for his list of pet hates."

"You've only got to mention anything remotely concerned with English literature," Daphne said, "or Greek, or Latin and even history, and he starts shouting. You know what I mean?"

Kim nodded ruefully. "Only too well. I come from a family of scientists, remember. I was the odd one out. They all regard me as useless, too."

"Sorry to add to your troubles, dear, but that's the way it is. So if he ever finds out about your degree . . ."

"I'd be out, is that it?"

Daphne nodded. "Anyway, as I told you yesterday, any time you feel you can't take it, I'll be here." She called to Candy, then said to Kim, "Life really is getting interesting with you next door. A bit like having a time-bomb ticking over. Don't leave yet, Kim, will you? I'd hate to miss the big explosion when you two have that stand-up fight I'm sure you're both heading for."

"Honestly, Daphne, I can't stick the man. We've had one or two minor skirmishes already."

"Glad to hear it. Owen wants keeping in his place at times. Although I must say, we've always got on well with him. He's got his good side, you know."

"He has?" Kim grinned. "You could have fooled me." But as soon as the words were out, she remembered his generosity towards her "financially embarrassed" parents, and her conscience pricked her. But she tried to soothe it by telling herself he must have had a motive, and a selfish one at that.

Candy came into the kitchen. She stopped dead at the door.

"Hallo, Candy," Kim said, feeling the child's astonished eyes on her.

"Trousers," muttered Candy. "None of the other ladies wore those."

"Didn't they?" asked Kim, her eyes seeking confirmation of the statement from Daphne.

"They were hardly the trousers type, either in character or physique," Daphne comented dryly. "Like me," she looked disparagingly at her bulges, "they didn't have the right measurements!"

Kim laughed and held out her hand. "Come along, Candy. Lunch."

Candy turned her head and walked past the outstretched hand. Kim made a despairing gesture, but Daphne shook her head. "Don't worry. She'll come round." But Kim doubted it very much.

They had their lunch in silence. As soon as it was over, Candy made for the door, but this time Kim stopped her. "You must stay with me this afternoon, Candy. Now I'm here you mustn't keep bothering Mrs. South."

"It's Auntie Daphne, not Mrs. South, and she says I'm not a bother, ever."

"All the same, I insist that you stay here. It's part of my job to look after you, dear."

The child's face grew scarlet. "I don't want to stay here!" she screamed, plunging headlong towards the door. "I hate you! I wish you'd leave, like all the others."

Kim, white with anger, stepped aside. "All right, go. You're just a disagreeable, bad-tempered little pest, so why should I want to keep you here? I don't like you any more than you like me. So you can go to your Auntie Daphne's, and stay there for all I care!"

Candy stared and began to cry. "The other ladies," she sobbed, "never said that."

It was as much as Kim could do not to put her arms round the child's shaking body and ask her forgiveness. Candy groped

47

for the door handle and went out.

Kim sank down and held her head. "Kiss her," her mother had said, "like I used to kiss you. She needs love." Yet all she had done was shout at her and drive her even further away.

Later, Kim went into the garden. She found a hoe in the shed and pushed dispiritedly at the earth along the flower-beds. She wished she knew more about gardening. She wished she knew more about housekeeping. She wished she knew more about children. She bent down to pull out some weeds.

Then Candy was standing beside her. Startled, Kim looked up. "I thought you were next door."

"I was. I saw you out here. I came back."

"Oh."

"Are you crying, Miss Kim?"

Kim kept her eyes down. "Of course not," she said. "It's – it's just my eyes watering a little."

"Oh. Like mine do sometimes."

Kim looked up and smiled through her tears. "That's right."

"I didn't know ladies' eyes watered, like little girls."

"Oh, they do, Candy. It's only natural."

"Yes," said Candy, and bent down to do some weeding, too. Kim showed her what to pull out and what to leave alone. They were silent after that, but it was a friendly silence.

Later, Kim said, "I'm going to make a cup of tea. Would you like one?"

"No, thank you."

"Lemonade?"

"Yes, please."

So they drank together in silence – a companionable silence.

For dinner that evening, Kim made a steak pie – minus onions – and put fresh fruit salad in jelly into the fridge to set.

Just before her employer was due to come home, she rushed upstairs to change. It depressed her to be wearing her mother's old dress again and it was with reluctance that she caught back her hair and twisted it into a bun, making herself look like an old-fashioned nanny.

But when Owen Lang came home, she might have been invisible. He did not even answer her murmured "good evening" when she placed his food before him.

"Back to normal", she thought with a mental shrug of hopelessness.

"You didn't say 'thank you' to Miss Kim, Daddy," Candy pointed out.

"Miss Paton," her father correctd, "not Miss Kim."

"All right, Miss Paton, then. But you still didn't say 'thank you.'"

Owen looked up at Kim as she stood at his side. "My daughter insists that I say 'thank you', Miss Paton." He bowed mockingly over his plate. "Thank you."

"That's all right, Mr. Lang," she answered evenly, moving to the door. "I didn't really expect thanks from you. I only associate good manners with well-bred people."

She enjoyed to the full her moment of victory until she felt the backlash of anger which darted like forked lightning across his eyes. She returned to the kitchen wondering how much longer he would tolerate her verbal insurrection.

She spent the evening in her bedroom and only emerged from it to tell Candy to get ready for bed. This time Kim did not offer to help. She returned to her bedroom and resumed her reading.

Some time later, when the silence from Candy's room grew so long Kim began to wonder why, she went through the door which divided the "family" part of the house from the "servants' quarters," and looked in at the little girl. She was sitting up in bed, hugging her knees, waiting.

"Why didn't you tell me you were ready?" Kim asked, her voice purposely sharp. She was not offering the child unwanted sympathy and warmth only to have it rejected.

Candy slid down into the bedclothes and Kim tucked her in.

"Goodnight," said Kim, and went to the door.

"Aren't you going to kiss me, Miss Kim?" asked a small voice.

What was she doing – egging her on in order to repulse her

49

again? "Not tonight. Last night you wiped it off."

"I won't wipe it off tonight, Miss Kim."

Kim opened the door and pulled it shut behind her.

"Miss Kim!" It was a shriek of appeal, muffled by bed-clothes stuffed into a mouth.

Kim went back. "Yes?"

Two blue eyes, wide with an unspoken plea, looked at her. "I won't rub it off tonight, Miss Kim." The child held her breath.

Kim bent down and put her lips to the soft pink cheek. It was not a kiss, but it was enough. With a sigh, Candy turned on to her side and closed her eyes.

Swallowing the lump that had somehow lodged itself in her throat, Kim sat in her armchair and stared unseeingly at the carpet. It seemed as though her tactics of alternating withdrawal with sympathy or fighting back as the situation demanded were paying off — with the daughter, if not with the father. Did they both share a deep-seated fear of being "chased" for their affections?

CHAPTER IV

Next morning Kim made sure she was the first downstairs, although Owen followed only a few minutes later. He looked round the kitchen.

"Where's my breakfast?"

"I've set the table in the dining-room, Mr. Lang."

"I always have my breakfast in the kitchen."

"I'm sorry, I didn't know."

"You didn't ask, did you?"

"I'll go and get the things," she offered, expecting him to say "don't bother, I'll have it in there for once," but he sat at the kitchen table and waited.

She served his bacon and egg straight from the cooker, piping hot. He took it without a word. She made some toast and then a pot of tea.

"I have coffee for breakfast, Miss Paton."

She said wearily, "I'm sorry, I didn't know."

He repeated, a little more sharply, "You didn't ask, did you?"

She was filled with a sense of inadequacy and her voice reflected it as she asked, "Do you want me to throw the tea away and make you some coffee?"

He considered her for a moment. "I ought to say 'yes' to teach you a lesson, but –" he looked at his watch, "that would make me late, so this time I won't. I'll have the tea."

"Yes, Mr. Lang," she said, with resignation.

While he finished his breakfast, she wondered what to do. She couldn't go upstairs in case he wanted something more. She couldn't sit at the table with him, because she supposed it would be against the rules for a housekeeper to breakfast with her employer, so she stood and stared out at the garden.

"Have you eaten, Miss Paton?" he asked sharply.

51

"No, Mr. Lang.'

"Then why the devil aren't you having your breakfast?"

She turned. "I didn't like to. I thought I'd better wait until you'd finished."

He said sarcastically, "Such consideration and respect from a housekeper! I'm simply not used to it. All the others just took it for granted."

She flushed angrily. He was putting her in the wrong again. There was no pleasing the man. She took her breakfast from the cooker and sat opposite him, eating it without enthusiasm, and wishing he would go to work and leave her in peace. She had never felt so uncomfortable. She was acutely conscious of him, even though he was not taking the slightest notice of her. She felt inferior and gauche and sighed with relief when he pushed back his chair and prepared to leave.

He heard the sigh and smiled sardonically. "Sorry to see me go, Miss Paton?"

She was about to nod her head politely when she saw the challenge in his eyes. "No, Mr. Lang. I'm very relieved, if you must know."

There was no irritation in his voice when he replied, "I rather gathered that. What more could I ask – a housekeeper who can't stand the sight of me?" He grinned and left her.

As soon as he had gone, Kim chased upstairs and changed into her sweater and slacks. She released her hair from its imprisoning bun and put on some make-up. It cheered her considerably.

Candy came down to her cereal and milk. She eyed Kim closely. "I told Daddy," she commented, "that you wore trousers."

"Candy, you didn't!"

She nodded. "He didn't believe me. He said he wouldn't allow a housekeeper of his to wear trousers."

"Oh, did he?" That was a challenge she had a very good mind to meet, except – except that she wanted to keep the job. Whatever happened, he must never find her in anything but her mother's old dress. She would have to buy another like it, so that she could wear them alternately.

That morning she went into the town. She told Candy, "You'll have to go into Auntie Daphne's this morning. I'm going to the shops."

"Oh." Candy thought for a moment. "Are you going by bus?"

"No. In my car."

"Oh. Then are you coming straight home?"

Kim shrugged, deliberately noncommittal. "I might have a coffee somewhere."

"Oh," again. Then, "Do you want me to come with you?"

"Not particularly."

Candy's forehead creased with disappointment. "Why, wouldn't there be room in your car?"

"Well," Kim hesitated, "it's only a very little car – but there might just be room – for you. Would you like to try?"

Eagerly, "Yes, I would. Shall I get my coat?"

Kim smiled to herself as she pulled out into the traffic with Candy beside her. She was learning a little more about children – and Candy in particular – every day. Only the father remained an enigma.

They went shopping, then they had coffee and a milk shake and chocolate biscuits at a café with a high counter and swivelling stools. When they got home, it was time for lunch. They ate it in the kitchen. They did not speak much – they never did. Speech did not seem necessary between them somehow.

The day passed and Candy did not once go into Daphne's house. She stayed in her bedroom playing with her dolls or reading.

"Haven't you any little friends to play with?" Kim asked her.

"One or two, at school. Not many. Daddy said I'm like him. He hasn't got many friends, either."

"I'm not surprised," Kim thought grimly. "With his personality, who would want to be a friend of his?" But again it came to her with a shock how alike father and daughter were.

That evening Kim was cooking the evening meal when she heard Owen's car turn into the driveway. She looked down at herself. She was still in trousers. She dropped everything and ran, reaching the landing as his key turned in the lock. She had never changed so quickly in her life. He called up the stairs that he wanted her.

"Coming, Mr. Lang," she answered, her voice muffled by the dress over her head. She grabbed her hair and twisted it back, took a paper tissue and scrubbed off the make-up and raced down the stairs, her heart pounding with effort, to face him in the dining-room.

He looked her over, eyebrows high. "What's the panic? You look like someone who's been caught in the act."

She tried to hide her guilt with a smile. "Sorry, Mr. Lang. But you did say you wanted me."

"Did I?" he said abstractedly. "It doesn't matter now."

"Oh." She sighed and turned away.

"I'm an absolute tyrant, aren't I, Miss Paton?" He was grinning. "I only do it to keep you on your toes – and to make you hate me."

She glowered. "You don't have to *make* me do that, Mr. Lang. It comes to me naturally."

He smiled lazily. "The point goes to you, Miss Paton. As they say in tennis – fifteen-love."

That evening, before it grew dark, she wandered round the garden. She really would have to read some gardening books. She was sure there were lots of things she should be doing out there. She pulled idly at a few weeds that were pushing their way between rose bushes, then dusted her hands and placed them on her hips, looking at the apple trees. She frowned, wondering if they should be sprayed. The roses – had they been pruned?

Without a sound, Owen appeared at her side. "You know a lot about gardening, Miss Paton? As much as you know about housekeeping?"

She looked up, her expression a give-away. Had he guessed? Had he caught her out at last? But his face told her nothing.

"First things first, I should say," he went on blandly. "The lawns – they need cutting." He looked her over. "Are you capable of using a lawn-mower? Have you the strength – the muscular strength? In that – elegant outfit you're wearing," she heard the sarcasm, "one could not even start to guess at your build, your physical attributes, if you have any – which I doubt."

She bit her lip, longing to retort, but held back. "Yes, I'll cut the lawn, Mr. Lang, if you'll show me where the mower is."

"I'll do better, Miss Paton. I'll get it out for you. Then I can stand back and watch you work."

The fierce look she turned on him made him smile. "Point in my favour, Miss Paton," he said softly. "Fifteen-all."

She mowed the lawn and he did watch her – from the kitchen window. But she didn't mind, she enjoyed the exercise. It brought a glow to her cheeks and she was breathing hard with effort when she asked him if he would please put the lawn-mower away.

He said, grinning, "That's helped you lose a few more inches, hasn't it? From the bundle you appear to be in that dress, it looks as if you could do with it."

She went upstairs, her head high. She told Candy to get ready for bed and the child did so without protest. Kim was sorting through her clothes when Candy tapped on the door and held out a comb. "Please will you do my hair, Miss Kim? The comb keeps getting caught."

Marvelling at what amounted almost to a declaration of dependence, Kim took the comb, trying not to pull too hard at the tangles. "Am I hurting, Candy?"

"A bit, Miss Kim, but I don't mind."

My word, thought Kim, this is progress. As she tucked the child into bed, she hovered over her uncertainly. Should she risk it? But Candy resolved the problem herself by reaching up and kissing Kim.

Kim's eyes grew moist, she couldn't help it, and Candy saw it, but she merely said, "Goodnight, Miss Kim."

"Goodnight, darling," whispered Kim, and went out.

"Miss Paton," came a voice from the hall, "are you coming down? I want to see you."

Now what? thought Kim. She answered, "Just coming, Mr. Lang."

She tugged at her mother's dress to tidy it, noticing with amusement how prim and strait-laced it made her look.

She found Owen Lang in the dining-room, working as usual. She folded her hands in front of her one over the other as she had seen housekeepers do on the stage, and asked, "Yes, Mr. Lang?"

His eyes seemed to register her docility and he raised an eyebrow. When he spoke, his tone was provocative.

"I understand from my daughter that you inveigled her into going shopping with you."

Kim's assumed meekness evaporated like dew in the morning sun. She unfolded her hands and clasped them tightly instead. "Inveigle implies enticement with evil motives, which is probably why you used the word." His smile increased her anger. "The truth is that she invited herself to accompany me, not the other way round."

"*Is* it the truth, Miss Paton? I can't see my daughter willingly going anywhere with someone she dislikes so much."

"You're a little out of date, Mr. Lang." She lowered her eyes. "Candy seems to like me now."

"She does?" Those hard blue eyes looked exaggeratedly incredulous. "You astonish me. Pardon me if I say I don't believe you."

Kim flared, "Ask your daughter, Mr. Lang." She looked down again. "Tonight she – she kissed me goodnight of her own accord."

"She did?" The incredulity was there again. "My word, I didn't know she was so hard up for affection."

"You, Mr. Lang," said Kim, choosing her words as though she had just learned a portion of the dictionary by heart, "are the most insultingly offensive man I have ever come across. You are also the most unfeeling, calculatedly callous creature I have ever had the misfortune to meet. And if you now want to dismiss me for insolence and insubordination, go ahead. It's given me such pleasure to express my honest opinion of you that it was worth risking dismissal to do it."

"My dear Miss Paton," he leaned back in his chair and smiled, "*dismiss* you? The thought never entered my head.

56

I'm enjoying myself. I'm also marvelling at your vocabulary, your command of the English language. Where did a simple-minded, half-educated housekeeper like you learn it all?"

The signals flashed, red for danger. She would have to keep better watch over herself, and stick to one syllable words. "I did attend school, like everyone else, Mr. Lang."

"And then – college?"

"College?" She started guiltily, then relaxed. "Oh, you mean technical college."

"Of course. What else did you think I meant?" He gave a cynical laugh. "Not, surely, an establishment of higher learning – a *university*?"

She laughed with him, but hers was a hollow sound. If only he knew! "Is that all, Mr. Lang?"

"No. I understand you went shopping in your own car."

"Of course. There was no point in travelling by bus, with my car ready and waiting."

"In that case, I'll have to make you a petrol allowance."

She was overwhelmed, once again, by his thoughtfulness. "It never occurred to me. It really doesn't matter."

"There she goes again, turning down the offer of extra money. I've never come across a female like you. Most of them are out for what they can get from an employer. You really will have to get yourself organised, Miss Paton." He smiled mockingly. "Anyway," he said, prepared to end the discussion, "a petrol allowance will be added to your weekly salary." He added, aiming to provoke, "But I don't have to worry. I won't be paying out thes *enormous* amounts of money to you much longer. Your time with us is running out fast. You've already been in my employ an inordinately long time. Three days, I believe? It surely can't last much longer!"

She closed her ears to the sarcasm and the bait. "Thank you for your generosity, Mr. Lang. I appreciate it." She hoped he caught the sincerity in her words. She could not tell because he kept his eyes on the papers in front of him. "Now is that all, Mr. Lang?"

He nodded and she left him.

Next day was Friday. "School on Monday," Kim reminded Candy gently, wondering what her reaction would be.

"Yes," said Candy flatly.

"Will you be glad to see your friends again?" Candy shrugged. "I expect you go to lots of parties," Kim went on, trying to get a response.

"No, I don't."

"Oh." Nonplussed, Kim gave up her questioning, but Candy said,

"I do get invited to parties, but Daddy won't let me go."

"Why ever not, Candy?"

"He says I can't give one back, so it's not fair if I go to other people's."

If Kim thought this hard on the child, she could not say so. She felt for the little girl, imagining the anguish she must suffer at being unable to share her friends' excitement as their respective parties approached.

Candy went shopping with Kim again. She did not seem to mind trailing round the supermarket collecting goods in the trolley. They met a few of her school friends walking round with their mothers. Candy smiled at them, transferring her smile upwards to Kim. There was a look in Candy's eyes which Kim could not understand, a look which spoke of pride and of possession.

Kim decided on cold meat and salad for the evening meal. She was preparing the tomatoes and slicing them when a car turned into the sideway. She dropped the knife, looked up at the kitchen clock on the wall, then stared down at herself. It couldn't be Owen. It was much too early. But if it was, she was caught red-handed, like a criminal, wearing trousers and a pink sleeveless top.

Somehow she must get up the stairs before Owen saw her. She dived along the hall as his key turned in the lock and was halfway up the stairs when he stepped inside.

He slammed the door and called her name, ordering her to come down. She ignored his order and continued upwards to the landing. But he was after her, dropping his briefcase on the hall floor and sprinting up the stairs two at a time.

"*Miss Paton!* I told you to come down!" She raced along the landing, through the dividing door which she closed every night on going to bed. She closed it now, but he forced it open against her, so she turned into her bedroom, but his foot was in the door, preventing her from closing it.

"Miss Paton," he growled, "will you stand still!" She did, with her back to him. "Miss Paton," his voice was quieter now, "will you turn round?"

She rotated on the spot and faced him, her face flushed, her breathing laboured from the chase. Her eyes held fright and fear of immediate dismissal. This, for him, she thought, must surely be the last straw.

He stared at her, his eyes travelling all over her, slowly, analytically, as if trying to discover a chemical formula that would fit her and explain her away.

"My God," he whispered, "what have I let into my house this time!"

"I'm sorry, Mr. Lang. I was just going to change, but –"

"You mean," he interrupted, "you were just going to assume your disguise, to shroud yourself in that horror of a dress, to continue your subterfuge, to keep up your pretence of being an innocent, prim, rather priggish young matron whose purity and virtue were beyond doubt."

She started to protest, but he went on, dwelling on the slim waist, the shapeliness above and below it, "This – this performance you've been putting on for my benefit is rather like a tantalisingly protracted unveiling ceremony." His tone became suggestive. "Now you really have me excited. When it's all over, what – enticements will I find underneath? How many more veils are you intending to remove, Miss Paton, before we get to the *dénouement*, the final inflaming revelation?"

She tried with her eyes to appeal for his understanding, but knew she was appealing in vain. She had to acknowledge that he was right. Slowly, subtly, he was unmasking her, uncovering her trickery, finding out for himself the deceptions she had used to get herself the job. She had no weapons with which to fight back, she could not satisfactorily answer his accusations.

She could only apologise and wait for the dismissal.

But it did not come. Incredibly he did not take out his cheque book and ask her how much he owed her for four days' service.

"I'll change, Mr. Lang. I know you don't allow your house-keepers to wear trousers. Candy told me." She turned. "I'll just go and change—"

But he stopped her flow of words. He snapped, suddenly irritable, "Wear what you like! Whatever I say won't stop you. You seem to have been doing exactly what you like ever since you set foot in my house." He looked her over again, as if he still could not take in the reality of the woman in front of him. He said slowly, "There can be no doubt about it, Miss Paton. You've won, game, set *and match*!"

Kim put her mother's dress away for the last time. In a day or so she would pack it up and send it home.

When Candy was in bed that evening, she asked her employer's permission to use the phone again. "I'd like to contact a — a friend of mine."

He regarded her closely. "By the look in your eye, it's a boy-friend. Am I correct?"

She answered resentfully, because he had no right to ask, "Yes, one of them."

"Of course," he smiled, "you have — how many? Three, isn't it? And this is a — special one?"

"Perhaps. He's a friend of my brother's. So are the other two."

"Your brother has a lot of friends?"

"Yes, mostly girl-friends."

"So, not to be outdone, you emulate your brother. You have a lot of boy-friends."

Why was he probing? It was no business of his. "It's not that I set out to get them . . ."

"They set out to get you?" He considered her in detail and said, "Seeing you now as you really are, that's not entirely beyond my comprehension."

"May I phone?" she snapped. "I'll pay for the call."

"I'll make quite sure of that," he came back blandly. "I shall deduct it from your salary."

She turned sharply and closed the sitting-room door. She dialled and waited, visualising John's cheerful open face, his light-brown hair and happy-go-lucky manner. She felt a spark of pleasure at hearing his voice. It was something familiar to cling to, something of her home surroundings and part of the happy environment she gave up when she decided, in a moment of madness, to take on this job.

"John? Kim here."

"I was wondering," John said, "when you were going to honour me with an explanation of your sudden disappearance. Did you have to leave me in the lurch without a word of farewell?"

"Sorry, John, but it all happened so quickly . . ."

"All right, don't bother to explain. I understand. I'm only a small pebble on your rather large beach."

"It's not that, John –"

He laughed. "What's all this Perry tells me about your employer being a wolf who goes round seducing women, including you?"

She laughed and it was such a relief that it occurred to her that she had not laughed wholeheartedly since she had left home. "Nothing could be farther from the truth, John. If only you knew!"

They talked for a while and rang off. She knocked on the sitting-room door and thanked her employer for allowing her to use the phone.

"I hope I wasn't too long, Mr. Lang."

He looked at his watch. "I timed you. You were exactly – er – sixteen and a half minutes. If you multiply that by three – one call to each boy-friend – and repeat the exercise often enough, it's going to cost you quite a lot of money."

She slammed the door, put on a cardigan and went out into the garden. It was dusk and the sweet scent of the spring flowers was heavy in the chill air. Daphne's husband was gardening. He looked up. He was, she saw, of medium height, tending to plumpness. He smiled, walked to the fence and extended his hand across the top of it. "How do you do? Hamish South," he said, "and you, I'm sure, are Miss Paton, the new housekeeper."

Kim nodded. "I've often admired your garden. How do you get it looking so good? Green fingers?"

He laughed. "Partly. Partly, also, because it's my hobby. I live and breathe gardening. Ask my wife!"

Kim looked round at Owen Lang's garden. "I wish I knew more about the subject myself." She looked over her shoulder at the sitting-room window and saw her employer standing, hands in pockets, watching them. She lowered her voice. "It's part of my job, but –"

"Miss Paton," Hamish interrupted, keeping his voice low, too, "if ever you need any help or advice, don't hesitate to ask. I'll be delighted to give it to you. Any heavy jobs you want doing, just tell me. Owen there," he nodded at the figure at the window, "hates gardening like a child hates having its face washed. I don't think I've ever seen him with a garden-ing implement in his hand. If it weren't for his housekeeper – I mean," he corrected himself with a laugh, "his succession of housekeepers, the place would be overgrown with weeds. The trouble is, they've all had different ideas of where things should be planted, and then someone else has succeeded them and the result is chaotic. Never mind," he said, after they had laughed again, "just ask me when you need to."

They said goodnight and went in. Owen was hovering at the kitchen door when she turned on the light.

"Getting friendly with the neighbours?" he asked with a sneer. "Or rather, the masculine half?"

"No," she snapped, "he was getting friendly with me."

"Of course," he came back, "that's your story, isn't it? As with your boy-friends . . ."

"Is there anything," she asked icily, "in my terms of em-ployment which prevents my getting friendly with the neigh-bours?"

"Just to remind you, Miss Paton," his voice was quiet, "they are *my* neighbours, not yours. Your stay here is so ephemeral it's hardly worth your while cultivating them, is it?"

Was the man quite unreasonable? "But Mr. Lang, even if, as you keep saying, I won't be here very long, if the people next door are nice enough to offer their friendship, why should I refuse it? I'm surely entitled to some friends of my own."

He looked down at the newspaper in his hand. "They happen to be my friends as well as my neighbours, Miss Paton."

"In other words," she tried to keep the dismay from her voice, "you're saying 'hands off'?"

"Exactly." He retreated into his sitting room.

The man was impossible, she told herself, and for the first time since her arrival found herself near to tears.

It was the weekend. Owen was at home for the next two days. Kim tried to keep out of his way, but at times they had to meet. He kept going into the kitchen while she was busy at the sink or the cooker. Sometimes Candy was with her, watching her making cakes and jam tarts. Somehow she would manage to get in her father's way and he would talk to her sharply.

On Sunday morning Kim was making Owen's bed when he walked in. He found something he was looking for on the dressing-table.

"Do you want me to go out, Mr. Lang?" she asked.

He became cynical at once. "Why? Do you think I've got designs on you?" He looked at the bed, then, insultingly, at her as if measuring her up. "Nothing was farther from my mind – until you put it there."

She drew in her lips and he smiled. "Carry on with what you're doing, Miss Paton. That's what I employ you for – nothing else."

She flushed a deep red and it seemed to give him immense satisfaction. Then he went out.

That afternoon, Hamish worked in his garden. Beside him, Daphne was weeding.

Over the fence Kim said, "Hallo."

They both responded immediately. "How's things?" asked Daphne, looking askance at Owen's windows to make sure he could not hear their conversation.

"Could be worse," answered Kim, her voice low.

"Keeping your head above water?" Hamish asked sympathetically. "Don't worry, we know how difficult Owen can be. He's a good friend of ours, but we know he's got a bad side as well as a good."

"Haven't we all?" commented Daphne.

Candy skipped into the garden. Daphne whispered, "She looks a different child these days. You must have worked some magic on her, Kim."

"Hallo there, Candy," Hamish called, "coming into my garden to help me, like you usually do?"

Candy looked at him, then at Daphne, then at Kim. Finally she shook her head. "Going to help Miss Kim today."

Daphne laughed. "*Miss* Kim? That sounds funny."

"All right," Candy said, with a frown. "I'm going to help *Kim*."

"That sounds better," commented Hamish, and went on with his digging.

Kim ventured, "Mr. South –"

"Hamish to you."

"All right, Hamish, should I be doing anything to the apple trees?"

He stopped immediately and considered her question. "Yes, the apple trees should be sprayed. I've been telling Owen that, but telling him anything about gardening is like asking the rain to stop falling. Makes no impression." He scratched his head. "It's not a job for you, you know. Not experienced enough." He looked at his wife. "Think Owen would object if I went round one evening and did it for Kim?"

Daphne frowned and looked apprehensively at her neighbour's house. "Ask him."

"Not on your life," answered Hamish. "Either I do it, and that's that, or I don't. If I ask him I'll only get a rude answer." He said to Kim, "Tomorrow evening all right? It needs a special solution and a special spray, which I've got and Owen hasn't."

"Thanks," said Kim, and she meant it, from the bottom of

her heart.

As Candy prepared for bed that evening, she took her comb in to Kim and held it out. She did not speak, she did not need to. Kim knew it was a gesture which tacitly demonstrated Candy's complete acceptance of her into the household.

It was also, to Kim, a little frightening. Kim knew, and Candy knew, that she was quite capable of combing her own hair, and such an action, premeditated and deliberate as it was, implied that the child was wilfully and determinedly becoming increasingly dependent on her. It was a realisation which made Kim's fingers jerk up to the neck of her blouse as if it were suddenly too tight for comfort and was threatening to choke her.

Later Candy called, "I'm ready." Kim went into her and sat on the bed. Candy's arms came up and closed round her neck.

"School tomorrow, Candy," Kim said.

Candy nodded. "When I come home," came the urgent, anxious whisper, "will you still be here?"

"But, darling," Kim answered, aghast, "of course I will be."

"And when I wake up every morning, will you still be here?"

Kim could only repeat, her throat tight, "Of course, of course."

"You won't be gone away for ever?"

Kim could only shake her head, unable now to speak. She kissed the pink cheek, whispered, "Sleep well," and went out.

Candy was down early to breakfast next morning. She was dressed in her grey tunic and white blouse.

"You look smart," Kim commented. "Have you far to go to school?"

Owen came into the kitchen, took his place at the table, opened the morning paper and waited for his breakfast.

"Yes," said Candy. "A long walk."

"Oh," said Kim. She put Owen's breakfast in front of him. "Would you like me to take you in my car, Candy?"

Candy's eyes opened, wide and expectant.

"My daughter will walk to school," came curtly from the man behind the newspaper. "She always has and while she attends that particular school, always will."

Candy's face fell.

"But, Mr. Lang," Kim argued, "it would only take a few minutes in the car . . ."

"If I had wanted her to go by car, Miss Paton," his eyes were steely, "I would have taken her myself long ago."

"Other girls' daddies take them to school," Candy murmured, in the tone of one who knew she had lost.

There was silence. Owen tackled his breakfast. Candy toyed with hers. Kim sat opposite Owen and picked up her knife and fork.

"Other girls' mummies take them to school," came another murmur, subdued and sad.

Kim raised her eyes involuntarily and met Owen's across the table. "Mr. Lang?" Kim asked, softly and appealingly.

The silence this time was brittle, waiting. The eyes which held Kim's became granite-hard. "My daughter will be walking to school, Miss Paton."

"Yes, Mr. Lang," Kim murmured, in the tone of one who knew she had lost.

Two appealing blue eyes were turned to Kim's, but Kim shook her head. "Sorry, Candy," she whispered.

A knife and fork clattered on to a plate. A chair was pushed harshly back and Owen Lang strode out of his own kitchen, leaving his breakfast half-finished. He picked up his brief-case, slammed the front door, reversed his car from the garage and went to work.

Kim pushed her plate away. She could not eat another mouthful. She felt ill with remorse. If Candy had not been sitting there, staring up at her, eyes wide with fright, seeking reassurance, she would have burst into tears.

Because of her stubborn persistence, she had driven the man from his own house, his own breakfast, and now he would go hungry for the rest of the morning. She was overcome with guilt and with a nagging anxiety which astonished her because, in disliking the man as much as she did, his welfare should not have worried her at all.

"Come on, Candy," Kim said, forcing herself to sound encouraging, "finish your breakfast, then you must be off. At least you won't have to walk all the way home and back at lunch-time."

"Yes, I will," Candy told her. "Daddy won't let me have school dinners. The housekeeper always has to give it to me."

"He *what*? But, darling, it must make you tired out."

Candy nodded.

"Look, Candy, if I give you the money to stay to school dinner, will you?"

"If you like," Candy agreed.

"And then," Kim whispered, "I'll come and pick you up after school. Would you like that?"

Candy nodded again, her eyes bright. "Like other girls' mummies?"

"Yes, darling, like other girls' mummies." Candy put her coat on. "I can't take you, because your daddy said I mustn't, but he didn't say I couldn't pick you up, did he? But, Candy," she touched her arm as she was going out of the front door, "let's keep it a secret, shall we? Our very own secret?"

Candy nodded and ran off.

Kim spent the day washing and ironing the clothes and tidying up generally. Later in the afternoon, she found her way to the school by following Candy's directions. She parked the car and waited with a group of mothers, watching anxiously in case Candy had forgotten their arrangement.

But she had not forgotten. She walked from the school building to the gates, surrounded by other children, her eyes raking the crowd of women clustered on the pavement outside. When she saw Kim amongst them, her anxiety was transformed into a brilliant smile and she broke into a run. She clasped Kim's hand and skipped across the road to the car.

Owen came home, but nothing was said. Kim set his food in front of him and gave Candy hers. As she did so Candy looked up at her and they exchanged secret smiles. Owen noticed and frowned suspiciously.

As usual Kim ate alone in the kitchen. When the meal was over, she went in to collect the empty plates. Candy followed her out, saying, "At school today, Kim, we had a lovely pudding . . ."

Too late, Kim shushed her. Her father had heard. Kim, holding the plates, froze at the expression in those hard eyes. Candy, realising what she had done, put her hands to her mouth.

Owen stood, slowly. "What pudding, Candy?"

Candy, too frightened to answer, looked up at Kim, who walked back into the dining-room and replaced the plates on the table. War had been declared.

"Your daughter had dinner at school today, Mr. Lang."

He asked curtly, "On whose authority?"

"Mine, Mr. Lang."

"At whose expense?"

"Mine, Mr. Lang."

She needed all the courage she possessed to meet the anger in those eyes. Was this the end?

"Because you were too lazy to provide her with a meal yourself?"

"I knew you would say that," Kim returned quietly. "No. Because the distance she has to walk to school is, in my opinion, far enough twice a day, let alone four times."

"Your opinion was not sought on the subject."

Kim found Candy's hand in hers. She did not answer the challenge. She told him, telling herself at the same time, 'I'm dismissing myself', "I also collected her from school this afternoon in my car."

He paled, strode round the table to confront her. Kim stepped back involuntarily, feeling Candy moving with her.

"You've challenged me, Miss Paton," he said, his tone controlled but his eyes blazing, "you've pitted your wits against mine. This time you've lost. You will get out of this room and you will get out of my house. For good.'

"You're dismissing me, Mr. Lang?"

"I am dismissing you, Miss Paton. You will leave in the morning."

"No!" screamed Candy, "no, no, *no!*"

But no one took any notice of her.

Kim, pale now as her employer, tried to free her hand from the child's, managed at last to pull hers away. But Candy hung on to her arm. "Kim isn't going. Kim isn't leaving!"

But no one heard her.

"All right, Mr. Lang, I've been dismissed. But now I'm no longer an employee of yours, I can tell you exactly what I think of you. In my opinion, unasked for though it is, you're not fit to be called a father. Your daughter is not only a motherless child, she is also a fatherless child. She is, mentally if not physically, an orphan. At every opportunity, you push her away. You cannot seem, you don't even try, to get down to her mental level." She dared to go on, despite his searing anger. "You live so much up in the academic clouds, you're so adult, so *old*, so superior, so unbending and inflexible where she, a small vulnerable child is concerned, she would be better off in a children's home where at least she would mix with others of her own age, and with adults who understood her requirements, than with you who regard her as nothing more than an impediment, a nuisance to be brushed from your path."

He made a violent movement towards her as if to silence her. Candy screamed and buried her face against Kim. With difficulty, Kim turned to go. "I'll pack tonight, Mr. Lang, and leave in the morning."

"*Take me with you*," Candy screamed, "I don't want to be left alone with *him!* *I hate him!*"

With a suddenness which frightened Kim, Owen grew slack as if he had been winded by a body-blow. He dropped into a chair, a hand to his head.

"You win, Miss Paton," he forced out. "You have my daughter on your side. You've alienated her affections from me, which none of the others thought of as a form of security for keeping their jobs. A subtle manoeuvre, and it's worked."

Kim tried to speak, but found the words would not come. She cleared her throat and managed, "It was no manoeuvre, Mr. Lang. What has happened was inevitable. There was a void in her life that had to be filled and it so happened that I filled it."

"Deny it if you like, Miss Paton, but I repeat," he raised his head with effort, "you made it come about. I should also like to say something else. I bitterly regret the day I first set eyes on you, the day I first heard your voice."

"Thank you for that, Mr. Lang," she did nothing to stop the tears that were running down her cheeks, "thank you very, very much."

And she broke away from Candy and rushed up the stairs to her room. But Candy was close behind and together they sat on Kim's bed and cried.

A long time later, when they had both stopped crying, footsteps climbed the stairs. Owen appeared at the bedroom door. He gazed at them both in silence. He looked like a man who after a violent struggle, had faced the inevitable and come to terms with it.

He said wearily, "I withdraw my dismissal. It seems I'm stuck with you, whether I want you or not. You obviously can't go now – not yet." He turned and went away.

CHAPTER V

HAMISH kept his promise and sprayed the apple trees. Owen strolled into the garden, wrinkling his nose in distaste. "Judging by the smell, you're using something with sulphur in it, Hamish."

"Quite right, Owen. That's the analytical chemist in you coming out. It's a solution that controls disease and pests. It should give you a better crop of apples."

Owen thanked him for doing it.

Hamish called down from the step-ladder, "I'm not doing it for you, old boy, I'm doing it for your housekeeper." He grinned down at Owen. "How could any man resist such magnetism, such charm?"

Owen turned on his heel and went in. Hamish made a face at Kim, who was standing just out of range of the minute drops of chemical solution he was spraying over the branches.

"That's torn it," Hamish said. "I only meant it as a joke, and now I seem to have upset him."

"That's not difficult," Kim muttered. "I'm doing it all the time. But thanks, Hamish, for doing what was really my job."

"My dear," commented Hamish, "if you think you can tackle this garden without help, and manage the house, the child *and* the father, then you'd better think again."

"But I took the job on with my eyes open, Hamish. I knew what I was doing."

"It's my opinion," Hamish said, stepping down the ladder, "that Owen expects too much of his housekeepers. No wonder they come and go with such frequency."

Later, Kim looked for Owen and found him as usual in the dining-room.

He looked up wearily from his work. "Yes?"

She stood with her hands clasped loosely in front of her. "I've come to apologise, Mr. Lang."

71

"For what?"

"For all those things I said about you yesterday. I'm sorry, very sorry. Thank you for keeping me on."

He shrugged irritably. "I had no alternative. There's no more to be said."

She went out. No more, she told herself, until the next time.

In the morning she asked as he was leaving, "Do you mind, Mr. Lang, if I take Candy to school in my car?"

He slammed out of the house without answering, but he had not said "no" so Candy went to school in Kim's car. She stayed to school dinner too, that day and every day after that – with her father's permission and at her father's expense.

A few evenings later, Kim bullied her courage into submission and braved her employer's wrath once again. She found him, surprisingly, in the sitting-room, relaxing in an armchair, his long legs stretched out, his head resting on a cushion, listening to music.

His eyes must have been closed because as he called to her to enter, his eyelids lifted slowly and she saw how tired he looked. A tenderness, a compassion stirred within her which, she told herself, she would feel for any human being who looked as weary as he did.

"What do you want, Miss Paton?" The words came from lips stiff with fatigue.

She began to back away. "It doesn't matter, Mr. Lang. It can wait."

"Is it important?"

"Not really, I –"

"Oh, come in and sit down until this music is finished."

Embarrassed now, disliking the feeling of sharing his private room, she found an upright chair and sat down, but he, irritable now, motioned her to the armchair opposite his. She sank into it and did her best to relax, but she could not entirely lose her tension. His eyes were closed again and in tranquillity he looked a different man, handsome, younger, the lines of anxiety smoothed away. His arrogance was gone, his expression, yielding to the beauty of the music, hinted at hidden founts of warmth and humanity.

Her feelings, as she watched him, puzzled her. There was something about the man that worried her, agitated her. He was not happy, she was sure of that. He seemed incomplete, friendless, forsaken . . . By whom? she wondered.

She remembered what Daphne had said about his bad side – and his good. She herself had experienced his unexpected gestures of generosity. If only his barriers were lowered now and then, if only he would let people in to share his private world, if only he would not insist on keeping her out, at arms' length, away from his innermost self . . . She checked her thoughts abruptly, frightened at where they were leading, re-alising how she had allowed herself to think in personal, sub-jective terms, of his relationship, not to others, but to herself.

"Know this music, Miss Paton?" The words came softly, the customary harshness gone from his tone. She started at the sound of his voice and was too taken aback to reply imme-diately. He opened his eyes.

"Isn't it," she asked him, "a Mozart flute concerto?"

"It is." His surprise was genuine. "Full marks." He closed his eyes again.

She looked past him through the french windows into the garden beyond, loving the colours of spring, the pink and white blossom, the scarlet tulips, the sun-yellow daffodils. She sighed softly and closed her eyes, too, claimed at last by the music.

As it ended, her eyes flickered open to find that he was watching her. She coloured and sat up, embarrassed at having allowed herself to be carried away by the peace of his sitting-room into believing it was hers to share.

He rose abruptly. "What did you want me for?"

She stood, too, back in her place as the paid retainer, the servant on call, the servile housekeeper.

"It's about my car."

"What about your car, Miss Paton?" He spoke like a man who was wondering what was coming now.

"Leaving it in the roadway, leaving the lights on all night, is running down the battery. I was wondering . . ."

"Haven't you bought a parking light?"

"No. I keep forgetting to get one."

He tutted and went to the window to stare at the little red car. "The vehicle is strident in colour and impudent in mien, just like its owner." He looked at her, smiling. "I know they say pets get like their owners. I didn't know, until now, that cars did, too."

She smiled back and it was like a rocket shooting up into the night sky and bursting into a multitude of brilliant colours. She held her breath as he stared at her. What was he thinking?

But his next words brought her down to earth and like a burnt-out rocket she lay spent on the ground.

"I know exactly what's coming." His tolerant good-humour was short-lived. " 'Can I be allowed to park my car in the sideway?' The answer's 'no'. Get yourself a parking light."

"But, Mr. Lang ..." She frowned uncertainly and he walked away from the window and flung himself in the armchair again, leaving her standing alone and wilting against the fading evening light. "Mr. Lang, every morning when I go out to my car, I'm afraid the battery will be flat and I won't be able to start it, then I couldn't take Candy to school and she would have to run all the way, and even then she would be late."

He turned his head and regarded the droop of her shoulders. She had the appearance of one who thought she was losing.

"You certainly lay it on thick, don't you? You summon all your arguments, and they become more emotional as you proceed, rising to a climax at the end which you think that even I, hard-hearted though I am, can't resist. All the same, the answer's 'no'."

"But, Mr. Lang," she wailed, "suppose it happened one morning that I couldn't take Candy to school —"

He sat up. "Look, Miss Paton, I've never really given you permission to take her to school."

"But you didn't say I couldn't. I asked you and you didn't answer."

"There are times, Miss Paton, where you're concerned,

when no answer is possible. Whatever I say, you flout my instructions."

She tried another argument. "But why should I have to keep my car outside at the kerb, when the sideway is empty, when there's parking space available? In making me keep my car in the road, you're treating me as an interloper --"

"Which you are."

"I'm *not*. I may not be a member of the family, but I am a member of the household. That's something you can't deny."

He put his hand across his eyes. He sat perfectly still. He did not even breathe. It was as though there was a violent struggle going on within him.

Eventually he stood and faced her. He was pale and controlled, but Kim could see it was costing him an effort. "All right, Miss Paton, you win. Once again. You're making a take-over bid for my house and, from the look of it, for the occupants, too." He walked towards her, hands thrust into his trouser pockets. "All right, you may have got *one* of the family under your spell, but by heaven, you won't be able to lure the other one into your web, to mesmerise me with your charms, considerable though they are. I'll make damned sure of that!" He said through his teeth, "Now get out of this room before I lay these two hands on you," he drew them from his pockets and showed her, "and -- and --"

She ran into the hall. "But my car, Mr. Lang?"

"Your car? You can park it in the garage, and I'll park mine in the sideway. That's what you want, isn't it?" And he slammed the door in her face.

A few evenings later Candy announced, "It's my birthday soon, Daddy. Can I have a party?"

The question seemed to make her father more irritable than usual. "You know the answer to that, Candy. It's out of the question."

"But," she wailed, "Kim said I could, so why can't I?"

"Did she?" Her father looked darkly at his housekeeper as she hovered in the dining-room doorway. "Then 'Kim', as you call her, had no right to make such a promise without consulting me first."

"It wasn't a promise, Mr. Lang, it –"

He interrupted, repeating with emphasis, "Without consulting me, Miss Paton."

Candy wandered off, disconsolate but resigned, having grown used to refusals over the years.

"Miss Paton," Owen said curtly, "come in and close the door." This she did. "Now, what's all this about a party?"

She felt uncomfortable as she usually did under his scrutiny. "It's just that – well, Candy says she never goes to parties because she never has one herself. Parties mean a lot to little girls, I remember that from my childhood, so I thought if I gave one for her –"

"If *you* gave one for her?"

"Sorry, I meant if *you* gave one for her, she would then be invited to other children's." He did not reply, he just kept on looking at her. She coloured and looked down, wishing his expression would stop registering a very male appreciation of her attractions and would tell her whether her appeal was affecting him. She went on, "I can imagine how she feels about being the odd one out. At her age, it must be terrible to see other girls dressed up for parties she hasn't been invited to, watching their excitement, yet never being part of that excitement herself."

"Sob stuff again, Miss Paton?" he murmured. "Emotionalism, highly coloured with sentiment, all designed no doubt to show me what a terrible father I am to deprive my daughter of the pleasures of the social whirl of infancy?"

She said, plaintively, after a few moments, "I only told her I thought you might let her have a party, nothing more." She ended lamely, "I intended asking you first."

"That was very thoughtful of you, considering it is my house, and she is, after all, my daughter. I suppose you realise," he went on, "that it would involve a considerable amount of work, both in preparation and the management of a houseful of screaming, squealing young females?"

She nodded. "I know what I would be letting myself in for, if you were to agree to her having a party."

"And yet you still suggested it?"

"Yes, Mr. Lang." She held his eyes steadily until he looked away.

"All right, Miss Paton, if you will stick your neck out, you deserve to take the consequences. In fact, you'll deserve everything you get. Tell me a few days beforehand, and I'll arrange to come home late – very late, when it's all over."

She turned towards the door, then paused. "Thank you, Mr. Lang, for being so kind and," a purposeful glint came into her eyes, "for offering your help."

He caught the sarcasm and smiled. "All the same, Miss Paton, I appreciate your gesture, although I suspect it is not entirely free from self-interest."

She came to life. "What do you mean by that? What exactly do you think I have in mind?"

He raised his eyebrows at her annoyance. "You would deny that your 'altruism' was born of a desire to impress me, to show me, perhaps, what a good stepmother you would make to my daughter?"

She faced him squarely. "Mr. Lang, if you think I'm nursing a secret wish to become your wife, then you're deluding yourself. Why you should be so – so conceited as to assume that every woman who comes into contact with you cherishes a hidden longing to be married to you, I can't even begin to guess. As far as I'm concerned, my only desire is that you should continue to be my employer for the length of time it suits me to be your housekeeper, and not a minute, not one single second longer!"

He murmured blandly, "I'm delighted to hear it."

She closed the door on his baiting smile. It was no use. Where he was concerned, she just could not win.

It was Mrs. Harker's morning for cleaning. She was late and when the telephone rang, Kim suspected the worst.

"It's my arthritis, dear," Mrs. Harker said. "I'm off to the doctor to get something for it. It's troubling me a lot these days."

Kim told her not to worry. "I'll do the cleaning myself. Yes,

I'll tell Mr. Lang you're sorry."

So Kim tackled the cleaning and welcomed a call from Daphne at coffee-time. Daphne told her Mrs. Harker often let Owen down.

"Whenever he was minus a housekeeper – which was pretty often! – I did the cleaning if Mrs. Harker didn't come."

"My goodness," said Kim, "he's lucky to have such a good neighbour!"

"He is, isn't he?" Daphne laughed. "But honestly, I couldn't bear the thought of him trying to do it. He wouldn't know one end of the vacuum cleaner from the other!"

As she left she said, "Hamish and I would like you to come in one evening for a chat. How about tomorrow?"

"That's very nice of you," Kim answered. "I shouldn't really, you know. An employee doesn't usually mix socially with the next-door neighbours!"

"Employee my foot!" commented Daphne. "With your qualifications and your family background, you shouldn't be here slaving away for an ill-tempered, rude young man like Owen. Don't think we don't like him – we do, very much, but his manner is hardly one to endear an ordinary acquaintance to him, let alone someone he employs. How are you getting on with him, by the way? You haven't come screaming to me yet, like the others."

"We – have our ups and downs. The other evening," she looked down at her hands, "he dismissed me."

"What? But you're still here. How did it happen?"

"I gave Candy the money for school dinner." She said defensively, "Well, I thought it was such a long way for the poor child to walk four times a day."

"You're right. It is. In the waiting periods between housekeepers, I used to give her her dinner. I just assumed you'd taken over from me. So he dismissed you for that?"

"And for collecting her in my car."

"But, my dear, that was very good of you."

"Unfortunately he didn't see it that way. Said I'd flouted his authority and I must go. I didn't, because Candy screamed at him and said she would go with me."

Daphne stared, unbelieving. "My dear, what a situation!"

"So," Kim shrugged, "he had to let me stay."

"Oh," said Daphne, "I can foresee trouble for Mr. Owen Lang, big trouble." She went to the door. "Anyway, you'll come tomorrow evening? You know, for a drink and a chat."

"Thanks, Daphne, I'll look forward to it."

It was accepted now that Kim took Candy to school and collected her every afternoon. Candy would hold her hand and swagger at her side, as if showing her friends that she too had a "mummy" person to look after her as they had.

Kim served the meal as usual that evening and Candy said to her father, "Why can't Kim come in here with us, Daddy? We have our breakfast in her kitchen, so why can't she have tea in our dining-room?"

Owen, momentarily nonplussed, looked to Kim for an answer.

"It's different, Candy," said Kim. "This isn't my house. I just work here."

"No, you don't," declared Candy, and there was an element of anxiety in her tone, "you *live* here. Like we do."

"But it isn't my home, darling," Kim said, urging her to understand.

"Yes, it is. It *is* your home."

Kim shook her head. "My home," she looked quickly at Owen, who was fiddling with his glass of water, "is a long way away."

"Is your daddy there?" Kim nodded. "And your — mummy?"

Kim noticed the odd hesitation and the trace of envy. So did Owen, who snapped, "Be quiet, Candy. Get on with your meal."

"And your mummy?" persisted Candy.

"And my mummy. Now have your tea, darling, as your daddy says."

Kim's heart was strangely heavy as she went up to her room that evening. Her family — she missed them. She was due for time off — overdue, in fact. She had not mentioned the subject to her employer, but she would, soon.

79

The phone rang just as she settled Candy down for the night. Owen answered. "Miss Paton," he called. "For you."

He looked at her oddly as he handed her the receiver. "Kim Paton here. Oh, Perry! Nice to hear you."

"Sure you're all right?" her brother asked. "I'm Perry, your brother, not John, or Ron, or Don."

Kim laughed. "I know, but it's still nice to hear from you."

"Thanks. I'll remember you in my will for that. I have one or two of your hangers-on waiting beside me to talk to you. John first."

"Kim?" asked John. She visualised his cheerful face. "I'm feeling neglected. Why no word?"

"Too busy. Do you know, I haven't even given you a thought!"

"That's right, butter me up!" They chatted for a while, then Perry came back. "Now Don wants a word."

She spoke to Don, fair, tending to plumpness but full of fun. Perry must have taken the receiver from him because Kim heard a low growl. Perry said, "Now Ron. I'm beginning to feel like a compère introducing comedy turns on the telly."

Kim heard a scuffle at the other end and imagined her boy-friends' mock indignation. She had a few words with Ron and rang off.

Owen must have been listening. He stood at the dining-room door. "Was that your boy-friend?"

"Er – actually I spoke to three." She counted. "First John, then Ron, then Don."

"You don't mean it?" He threw back his head and laughed. He really laughed, for the first time since she had known him. "They rhyme. Thank heavens my name isn't Con – short for Conrad – otherwise you might feel the urge to add it to your list!"

She smiled weakly, but even that faded as he went on, "Good heavens, how do you deal with them? Make them queue up for your favours? Do you – take them in rotation?"

She flushed at the insinuation. "They're not boy-friends in the accepted sense of the word. They're just – well, friends."

"Oh, are they?" She hated the look in his eyes.

"But the person you spoke to was my brother."

"Was it? He sounds pleasant. Is he younger than you?"

"No, he's older. He's twenty —" she stopped, aghast at what she had nearly given away. Twenty-nine, she was supposed to be, the age she had given the agency woman.

Owen's eyes inspected her confusion with interest. "He's —?"

"I forget," she said sullenly.

"As sudden a case of amnesia as I've ever seen," he commented sardonically. He shot at her, "How old are you? I want the truth." She was silent. "Another veil about to be discarded, Miss Paton?" Still she said nothing. "Just to remind you," he persisted relentlessly, "you are alleged to be twenty-nine."

"That's what I told the employment agency, Mr. Lang."

"M'm. I commend your astuteness. A neat sidestep. All right, I see you've shut up like a clam. I won't pursue the subject."

"Goodnight, Mr. Lang," she said politely, hoping he would let her go. He did.

Mrs. Harker phoned again next morning. She wouldn't be coming any more, she said. "Doctor won't let me, dear. It's my arthritis playing me up. I'd only make it worse, he says."

When Kim gave Mrs. Harker's message to Owen on his return from work he said, "What now? Advertise for someone else?"

"I'll do it," Kim offered cheerfully. "I did it yesterday. I don't mind."

He looked at her, seeming puzzled. "I honestly don't know what to make of you. The more I get to know you the more astounded I become. All the other women I've employed as housekeepers would have downed tools by now and threatened to leave if I hadn't acquired the services of another cleaner on the spot. I'm actually beginning to believe the eulogies contained in that reference I received about your character and capabilities."

She coloured uncomfortably. What would happen, what

would he think of her, if he ever discovered the truth about that "reference"?

He continued to look at her speculatively. "There's something about you that's different. I can't put my finger on it, it's elusive and it tantalises me. A bit like a hypothesis which doesn't give the result you know it damned well ought to give. As a scientist, and I hasten to add, purely as a scientist, I'm fascinated by you."

Kim grew afraid as his keen analytical eyes seemed to be trying to break her down into component parts the better to uncover and divulge the very essence of her being. She was used to the eyes and probing minds of scientists, having lived among them since she was born, and had consequently grown to respect and perhaps even a little to fear them.

Her discomfiture increased as his gaze became less scientific and more masculine. She became conscious of her slacks, now grubby and in need of a wash, her untidy black hair which she had been too busy to comb for hours, and her lack of make-up which she had not had time to put on. Why did she have to look so unkempt and unattractive every time he saw her?

"You realise," he said, his eyes still busy with her and apparently enjoying her embarrassment, "that if you now take on the job of cleaning the house, I shall have to put up your wages again?"

She knew better now than to argue with him. She would have been quite happy to include the work in her normal duties, without extra pay, but she realised that if she told him so, he would deliberately twist the truth and imply that she was doing it with another motive in mind.

"As you wish, Mr. Lang." Just before she left him, she remembered to say "thank you".

As she settled Candy down for the night, she told her she was going to Auntie Daphne's house for a little while. Candy made a face.

"I won't be far away, will I? Only next-door. I'll pop in now and then to make sure you're all right."

That seemed to satisfy Candy and she settled down after

the usual goodnight kiss.

Kim changed and looked in the mirror, and for the first time since she had left home, she felt satisfied with her reflection. The tulip red of her dress, with its long sleeves caught into a band at the wrists, contrasted well with her jet black hair. The matching belt with its large gilt buckle emphasised her slim waist and the gold necklet which she clipped round her throat added interest to the low-cut neckline.

She pulled on her coat and crept downstairs, hoping she would not meet her employer. She did not want to tell him where she was going, in case it annoyed him. The Souths were really his friends, not hers. He would not miss her because she usually shut herself in her room every evening and he did not disturb her after that.

The Souths gave her a warm welcome. "Did you tell Owen you were coming?" Daphne asked.

"I didn't like to."

"We didn't tell him, either. But he'll soon know. He's coming in himself."

Kim went scarlet. "Daphne! How could you! And then not to tell me!"

"No, we didn't because we knew what your reaction would be." She looked at her husband. "And we were right, weren't we, Hamish?"

He laughed and nodded. "Anyway, while you're here, Kim," he said, "you're our guest, not Owen Lang's housekeeper. Let's try to forget your 'humble' position in life."

As Kim sat in one of the comfortable russet-coloured armchairs, the doorbell chimed. Hamish opened the door. She heard Owen's voice and grew tense at once.

"Relax, Kim," Daphne urged. "He won't eat you."

He appeared, smiling, but when he saw the South's other guest, sitting taut and anxious in the armchair, he stopped, stunned into stillness. Hamish was behind him, blocking the way, as if ready to cut off any threatened retreat.

"Go on in, old boy, make yourself at home." He rested his hand on Owen's shoulder and urged him forward. "May we introduce," he said with a broad grin, "a new friend of ours,

Kim Paton? Kim, Owen Lang."

Owen bowed stiffly. "Good evening, Miss Paton."

She murmured, flushing, "Good evening, Mr. Lang."

"Oh, for crying out loud!" exclaimed Hamish. "You're our guests. You're here on equal terms. Owen, she's Kim. Kim, he's Owen. Drop the formality, or we'll put you both outside the door."

Kim smiled, but Owen did not. He sat in the armchair opposite her, while Daphne and Hamish sat on the couch. He took the cigarette which Hamish offered him and Kim stared.

"He doesn't smoke at home?" Hamish asked Kim, offering Owen a light from his lighter.

Such a question implied an intimacy between them which simply did not exist. "Er – no, I haven't seen any evidence of it."

Daphne laughed. "Perhaps he does it behind locked doors. You know, a secret vice."

Owen drew on his cigarette, lowered his eyelids slightly and exhaled. "I smoke," he said, looking at Kim through the temporary haze he had created round himself, "in moments of stress, extreme concentration or when the answer to a difficult problem is eluding me."

"And what is the cause now?" Hamish joked, watching Owen eyeing Kim. "All three?"

Owen did not answer, but Daphne said, trying to get a reply, "The third, I should guess."

At last Owen said, with studied vagueness, "My life is beset with problems."

"Your biggest, no doubt," commented Hamish, leading him on, "being the young lady sitting opposite you at this moment."

"The biggest," Owen took him up, "being how to keep a housekeeper working for me for more than a few weeks at a time."

"There's one answer to that, boy," chuckled Hamish, "and one only. Marry one of them."

"Thanks for the suggestion, Hamish," Owen said, flicking ash into the ash tray at his side, "but it's not on. The sort of woman I employ as my housekeeper is not the sort of woman I would want as my wife."

"Not intelligent enough, eh, Owen?" He tapped his head. "Not enough of the old intellect?" He winked at Kim.

"Owen's second wife —" Daphne began.

"Which I have no intention of taking," Owen interposed.

"Would," Daphne continued, "have to pass an exam, an intelligence test, before he allowed himself to propose to her. He would have to make sure her mental ability was equal to his."

"I told you before," Owen said with a cynical smile, "all the clever women are ugly and all the beautiful ones are ignorant and stupid."

The Souths were enjoying themselves. "And never the twain shall meet, eh, Owen?" Hamish asked, walking to the sideboard and pouring out drinks.

"Never," said Owen, stubbing out his cigarette and taking a glass from his host, "never in my experience."

"Let's change the subject," Hamish said, handing Kim a drink and looking at her with a wicked gleam in his eye, "let's get Owen on his soapbox. Let's talk about the arts, about historians, the classics, English literature."

Owen held up a cautionary hand. "If you want me to remain sweet-tempered, Hamish, keep off that subject."

Kim found her voice, but it came out a little hoarse. "Is there something wrong with English literature, Mr. Lang?"

"Hey," said Daphne, "I thought it was going to be first names all round?"

Kim coloured, but still could not bring herself to call her employer by his first name, although she knew she would have to before the evening was over.

"No, Kim," came from Owen. She glanced at him and looked away, feeling her heart behaving oddly as he said her name. "There's nothing wrong with English literature as such, but speaking as an incorrigible scientist, I can't for the life of me see any point in studying it as a subject on its own, within the context of the technological age we're living in. What use is it, what application has it to present-day needs? What for

85

instance, can an English literature graduate do with his –"

"Or her –" interrupted Hamish, grinning.

"Or her – usually her," agreed Owen, "degree once she's got it. Virtually nothing, except teach, and in so doing create other literature graduates, who graduate, then teach, and so on *ad infinitum*."

"You mean they're self-perpetuating?" Daphne asked.

"Self-spawning," Owen said, with derision.

Hamish grinned again. "Over to you, Kim."

She frowned, wishing Hamish would stop playing cat and mouse with her. What could she say in defence of her own subject? Hadn't she tried time and again without success to get herself a job, outside teaching, suited to her qualifications? Wasn't there some truth in what Owen was saying?

"What's wrong with teaching children English literature?" she asked lamely.

"A great deal," Owen said, "when you consider *how* it's taught, how it's forced down their throats." He leaned back in his chair and accepted another cigarette, getting it going with Hamish's help. His eyes challenged Kim's. He said, "They should take it out of the school curriculum," and waited for her response.

His provocative statement spurred Kim at last to defend her own subject. "But that's ridiculous! How can children learn about their literary heritage if they aren't taught about it at school?"

"Kim," Owen leaned forward, "look at it this way. What an adult reads or does not read is as private and personal a matter as the religion he does or does not practise. So, in my opinion, it's unforgivable to compel the young – who can't argue with their teachers – to read those lengthy and out-of-date pieces of writing called the 'classics', to dose them with the stuff like nasty medicine, on the grounds that if they don't 'drink it up' like good children, they can't be regarded by society as 'properly educated'."

"You simply can't dismiss the classics like that, Mr. –" She pulled herself up sharply and forced herself to say, "Owen." The mere use of his name seemed somehow to bring him

nearer, to make him more approachable, more human, more
– much more likeable.

"The so-called classics, Kim," she was conscious of the
intense interest of their host and hostess, "were written for
their times and not with posterity in mind. They were written
in the idiom and the style of their time."

"Then surely the fact that they've lived on beyond their
times," Kim pointed out, "proves their greatness?"

"I'm not questioning that," Owen said, "but why should
children be forced to read page after page of outdated prose
which, if they were to copy the style in their own writings,
would be dismissed by the teacher as hopelessly out of date in
this age of short sentences and pithily written ideas?" He
leaned back. "The day educationists insist on children being
compelled to read scientific books as part of their cultural
heritage, as they are now made to read the classics, then I
might agree to tolerate the compulsory study of English literature."

"Useless types, arts graduates, eh, Owen?" Hamish
laughed.

Owen drew on his cigarette and smiled through the smoke
he had released. "Ought to have been strangled at birth."

Hamish laughed out loud and Daphne nudged him. Kim
felt she was sitting on a cushion stuffed with drawing pins.
What was Hamish up to, leading Owen on like that? He knew
– Daphne had obviously told him – that she was an arts
graduate herself. Suppose Owen guessed her educational background? Suppose he now began to suspect the truth, that she
was a sham, and was just acting a part?

"So arts graduates," Kim remarked, as casually as she
could, "are something else I shall have to add to your list –
your long list – of pet hates, Owen?" Again she forced out his
name.

He smiled, as if guessing her struggle. "They are."

"So, Owen," Hamish said, "you wouldn't marry an arts
graduate at any price, any more than you'd marry your housekeeper?"

"Absolutely not," agreed Owen blandly.

"No matter how intelligent she might be?"

"She couldn't possibly be intelligent. She wouldn't be an arts graduate – or a housekeeper – if she were."

"And I," Kim retaliated through her teeth, "wouldn't marry a scientist if I were offered a fortune to do so!"

"And what," Owen asked the glowing tip of his cigarette, "does Kim Paton know about scientists?"

Kim darted a look at Daphne, who was frowning, then at Hamish, who was grinning.

"Well," she said, "I – I've met one or two."

Owen leaned forward as if the subject intrigued him. "And what did you find so repulsive about those scientists that it put you off the breed for life?"

Kim, feeling painfully disloyal to her family, had to hunt around in her mind for objections. Then she thought of her employer and this helped her considerably. "Their arrogance, their assumption that they can never be wrong and that all the rest of the world are fools. Their obsessive conviction that they are born to be the world's rulers . . ."

Hamish was rocking with laughter. He croaked, "Their hatred of arts graduates?"

"Yes," muttered Kim, glowering at her employer and antagonist.

Daphne patted her husband's knee and said diplomatically, "Time we got the food."

"Right." Hamish stood and pulled his wife to her feet. "Excuse us, you two. Just make yourselves at home. Carry on with the discussion. If you get too – er – entangled and want a referee, I'll come in and part you." He laughed again and his wife led him out quickly.

There was a long and difficult silence, broken only by the clatter of crockery from the kitchen and the chatter of their host and hostess. Embarrassed to the point of incoherence and desperate for something to do, Kim wandered to the window and gazed out into the garden.

She heard Owen move and her skin prickled. He came to stand beside her. He did not touch her, yet her body throbbed as though he had.

He said conversationally, "You like gardening, Kim?"

Caught off-guard, she answered, "Not particularly. I don't know much about it."

She drew in her breath and gazed up at him, her eyes wide with anxiety.

He murmured, smiling like a man whose trick had worked, "Another veil about to fall? Another lie you've told me?"

She began, mustering her indignation like a soldier loading bullets into a rifle, "I didn't lie –" but stopped, remembering her addition of six years to her age, the false reference, her misrepresentation of her parents' financial status.

"Go on," he said softly, "look me in the eye and tell me you haven't lied to me, then I might believe you."

She looked into his eyes. The evening light was fading and his back was to the window. It was too dark to see his expression, to tell what he was thinking. If she told him the truth this would be where they parted company. This, for her, would be the end of the road, and she would never see him again.

CHAPTER VI

THE door opened and Daphne pushed in a trolley laden with savouries, sandwiches and coffee.

Owen bent down and whispered, "Saved by the bell, Kim."

Light flooded the room as Hamish flicked the switch and Kim blinked and swayed, swamped by relief and a feeling of reprieve. She groped her way back to the armchair. She needed time to recover from the revelation of yet another of her secrets, from the odd behaviour of her heartbeats and from the escape she had had from having to tell her employer the truth.

She remembered Candy and stood up. "I'll just look in next door—"

"Sit down," Daphne said. "I popped in myself and she's fast asleep and looking like an angel."

Kim thanked her and glanced at Candy's father. He was stirring his coffee thoughtfully. "I have a very conscientious housekeeper."

"I am glad you realise it," Daphne retorted. "You should cherish that girl. You won't have her for ever, you know."

"I'm aware of that," he said quietly. "I have no intention of keeping her 'for ever', as you put it. With the explosive situation which exists between us, at any time she might dismiss herself, or – more likely," he smiled provocatively at Kim, "I might dismiss her."

"Some men," murmured Hamish, as if to himself, "don't know when they're lucky."

After that, the evening passed pleasantly. Kim saw a new side to her employer. She had not dreamed he could be so entertaining and amusing and so – likeable. She was sorry when he glanced at his watch and said they must go.

As Daphne and Hamish saw them out, Daphne said, looking pointedly at them both, "We shall expect to be asked back to your place soon."

Kim looked away, having no answer. It was not for her to say she would be delighted to invite them. "Certainly," said Owen promptly. "I shall advise my housekeeper of the date and time and instruct her to provide the necessary eatables."

Hamish added, with a wicked smile, "And ask her to act as hostess."

"That," said Owen, looking down at Kim, "remains to be seen. We may not be on speaking terms that evening."

They laughed and waved and Kim and Owen walked side by side into the darkness. Kim tripped over a paving stone and Owen's arm came out to support her. "It's the first time," he murmured, "I've known anyone get drunk on coffee."

She laughed, liking the feel of his arm round her waist. He opened the front door and as soon as they stepped inside, the situation returned to normal.

"Goodnight, Mr. Lang," she said in a businesslike voice.

"Goodnight, Miss Paton," he replied in the same tone, and they parted.

There was a certain strain in the atmosphere at breakfast-time next morning. Deep down, Kim resented being relegated to her place of the docile domestic servant, but she told herself she was being unreasonable to expect anything else.

Owen was sharp to the point of rudeness and she could only assume he was afraid she would forget her place because she had been treated as his equal last night. When he left for work she gave a sigh of relief and Candy unconsciously echoed it.

But all day Kim found herself thinking about him, how pleasant he had been at the Souths', how he had lost his reserve and treated her as a human being instead of an unthinking automaton.

Nothing had changed by the time he returned that evening. His manner was formal and it was as though the evening before had never been. After settling Candy into bed, Kim retired to her room with relief, glad to escape from his curtness.

She selected a volume of poetry from her bookshelf and

curled up on the bed, her legs tucked under her. She turned the pages idly, reading the poems here and there, trying to catch the elusive meanings behind the imagery which the poet had written into the verse.

Her eye was caught by some words, her imagination wandered as she read them, and into her mind came the picture of a man. As she recognised the face she almost shut the book with shock and panic. She read,

> *"For the one I love most lay sleeping by*
> *me under the same cover in the cool night,*
> *In the stillness in the autumn moonbeams his*
> *face was inclined toward me,*
> *And his arm lay lightly around my breast – and*
> *that night I was happy."*

Her throat contracted as her fingers clutched at it, her head dropped back against the wall behind her, her body throbbed as it came to her what had happened, and she could not, would not acknowledge that it was true.

There was a tap on the bedroom door. Unthinkingly she called "Come in", assuming it was Candy wanting her.

He came into the room and she thrust the book behind her, confused, dumbfounded that he should have come to seek her out.

The thump of her heart was hurting her now and she tried in vain to regain her composure. He saw her confusion and misinterpreted it.

"I imagine," he said, strolling across to her, "that you're reading something you don't want me to see."

He had imagined right, she thought.

"Is it, perhaps, one of those paperbacks with a lurid picture on the cover which utterly misleads about its contents? Is that why you've hidden it?"

She tried to laugh, but it was a feeble effort. She shook her head.

"Then why are you hiding it?"

"Do you want to see me about something?"

"Don't change the subject, Miss Paton. You won't succeed

in diverting me." He held out his hand. "May I? I promise not to condemn you for your low literary tastes."

She handed the book over. She had no alternative. He saw the title, he saw the name of the poet. He frowned and looked at her.

"*Leaves of Grass* by Walt Whitman? You read him? How come?"

How could she tell him without giving her secret — her most important secret — away? She shrugged. "He interests me."

He read the details aloud. " 'Walt Whitman, born 1819, Long Island, U.S.A. ... In 1873 settled in Camden, New Jersey, where he died in 1892.' "

He turned the pages and a poem must have caught his attention because he stopped and read it through. He looked for a chair and sat down. "This," he said, "I like. This is most appropriate. Shall I read it to you?"

Without waiting for her answer, he did.

> " '*Are you the new person drawn toward me?*
> *To begin with, take warning, I am surely*
>   *far different from what you suppose;*
> *Do you suppose you will find in me your*
>   *ideal?*
> *Do you think it so easy to have me become*
>   *your lover?*' "

He whispered, "Well, Miss Paton?"
She looked away, her cheeks on fire. He went on,

> " '*Do you think the friendship of me would*
>   *be unalloy'd satisfaction?*' "

He asked softly, "Do you, Kim?

> " '*Do you think I'm trusty and faithful?*
> *Do you see no further than this façade,*
>   *this smooth and tolerant manner of me?*
> *Do you suppose yourself advancing on real*
>   *ground toward a real heroic man?*
> *Have you no thought, O dreamer, that it may*
>   *be all maya, illusion?*' "

He closed the book, murmuring, "Well, Kim, what is your answer?"

"There are so many questions, Mr. Lang," she whispered, "how can I answer them?"

"Simple. To some the answer would be 'no', to others, 'yes'."

She tried to deflect his attention. "Do you ask all your housekeepers such questions?"

"I can answer *your* question unequivocally. No. None of my other housekeepers ever read Walt Whitman."

She smiled. "Then it's hardly fair to expect me to answer them, is it?"

"Well played, Miss Paton!" He handed the book back to her. "But it would have been of the utmost interest to me to have heard your answers." As the book passed between them, a piece of paper fell from between the pages and fluttered to the floor.

She uncurled her legs and dived for it, but she was too late. He reached it first.

"What's this? Another poem? Not Whitman again? Ah, no, an Englishman this time — Robert Herrick." He read it to himself and looked at her closely. "What *lucky* man did you have in mind when you so painstakingly copied out this declaration of love?" He quoted,

> " 'Thou art my life, my love, my heart,
>   The very eyes of me:
> And hast command of every part
>   To live and die for thee.' "

He gave her back the piece of paper. "So there is a man in your life, a very special man?"

"Not really." She slipped the paper back into the book. "I told you, I have a number of boy-friends. I just thought it a beautiful piece of writing."

"Hoping one day to find a man who would merit it, no doubt?"

"Perhaps," she said evasively.

"And have you met him yet?"

94

Was she about to tell him another lie? She shook her head slowly.

"Never mind," his tone was falsely sympathetic, "just keep on hoping. You may meet such a man. Although at your age — twenty-nine, isn't it?" he raised a sceptical eyebrow and smiled, "you must be aware surely of the passing of time?"

Her eyes were dull as she asked him again, "Do you want to see me about something? Will you please tell me what it is and —"

"And get out?" He smiled. "All right, message received. I can take a hint, even from my *illiterate* housekeeper. The day after tomorrow I'm bringing home a colleague for the evening. We have some business to discuss. Could you provide an appropriate meal?"

"Of course."

"Good. And thanks." He wandered to her bookshelf and inspected her reading matter. "Well, well. My ignorant, half-educated housekeeper has the taste of a classicist. Richardson, Fielding, Chaucer — in the old English, too — Samuel Johnson, Jane Austen, George Eliot, the Brontës, not to mention poets and dramatists of all shapes and sizes." He turned, his eyebrows lifted provocatively, the wave of his arm indicating the contents of the bookshelf. "What is all this — this façade? Did you raid a secondhand bookshop and fill up a suitcase with books and stagger here with them to display them with the intention of impressing me with your sham learning?"

She could not answer his accusations, because she would have had to tell him the truth about her university degree. And that above all she had to keep to herself. So she remained silent, allowing his words to go unchallenged.

"Now if," he smiled baitingly, "these were books on science, I should be mightily impressed. "If," he drew out one of the volumes, "you had any leanings towards science, any at all, I might," he idly turned the pages, "revise my vow that I would never marry any of my housekeepers. In fact, I would go so far as to say that if your scientific knowledge equalled your physical attractions," he was speaking softly, casually, almost to himself, "you would be a dream come true." He did not say whose dream.

His tone hardened. "Of one thing I am certain – my daughter, when she grows up, is going to be a scientist. None of your literary nonsense for her."

"But, Mr. Lang," Kim sat up, her back rigid, aghast at his dogmatic approach to his daughter's education, "you can't make an unqualified statement like that. How do you know yet where her abilities lie?"

He replaced the book on the shelf. "Her abilities, Miss Paton, are damned well going to lie in the scientific field. I'm not open to argument on the subject. My mind is made up."

"But, Mr. Lang, she might want to be an artist, a teacher of English, an historian. She might be hopeless at scientific subjects . . ."

She saw that she had angered him. He repeated slowly and clearly, "She is going to be a scientist, Miss Paton. I will have no arts graduate, no literary types in my family. Their very existence in this age of technology is an anachronism. And what's more, the few occupations which are open to them, apart from teaching, are hopelessly overcrowded and competition for any vacancies is high."

She could confirm all he was saying by her own experience, her own miserable failure to get the jobs she had applied for in her own particular line.

She said, "If you persist in trying to dictate to your daughter what she should or should not do with her life, I can tell you one thing for certain – she'll rebel. If she has any spirit, and I know she has, she'll go the other way. I know by experience –" She stopped abruptly.

He raised his eyebrows. "By experience, Miss Paton?"

She had nearly given herself away again! "By – by watching others, other families, other – other girls of my own age. When pressure has been applied to them in one direction, they've gone the other."

She looked at him apprehensively. Had she put him off the scent? His face gave nothing away except that he seemed angry, perhaps at being opposed by his "half-educated" housekeeper, and on a subject that was his concern and his only – his daughter's future.

He reminded her curtly that he would be having a visitor to dinner the evening after next and left her at last.

She wandered round the garden the following afternoon, knowing there must be a number of jobs waiting to be done. Daphne saw her and came out. "How are things?"

Kim shrugged. "So-so. Same as before. We had a bit of an argument about Candy's future yesterday evening –"

"My dear, if you argued with him about that, it's a wonder you still possess a head and that he didn't snap it off. To challenge him on his own ground – and about his own child!"

"He did snap my head off, but I snapped back." Kim frowned. "I suppose it was cheek on my part. Candy's future is his business after all, not mine. All the same . . ."

"Give it up, dear. There's enough cause for trouble between you without looking for it."

Kim gazed disconsolately round the garden. "I was wondering if Hamish . . ."

"Would tell you what to do about the garden? But of course. He'll be out here again this evening, so you can catch him then."

Later, when Hamish was busy mowing the lawn, Kim called to him. He leaned on the fence and surveyed Owen's "estate" as he put it. "Now those roses," he pointed, "they should have been pruned long ago. It breaks my heart to see them growing rampant." He looked at her. "Know how to do it? No? Right, I'll get my secateurs and come right in. Owen anywhere about? Too bad if he is. I'm inviting myself in, I'm not asking permission."

He came in through the side door.

Kim said, "I think I'll copy you and mow the lawn. Would you mind, Hamish, lifting the mower out of the shed?"

He did so, and Kim cut the grass while he pruned the roses. "That clematis, it needs cutting back too," Hamish commented, going across to the plant which was growing against some trellis-work fastened to a wall of the house.

As Kim moved the lawn mower backwards and forwards over the grass, she felt she was being watched. She glanced towards the house and saw that Owen was standing at the french windows, which he had opened wide. She could see from his sardonic expression what he was thinking – that she had coerced Hamish into doing the gardening for her.

She left the mower and whispered to Hamish that Owen was watching them. "Let him," Hamish said, "I'm doing this voluntarily. If he doesn't like it, he should learn how to do it himself."

As he talked, they heard the sound of the lawn-mower in motion. Kim turned guiltily and could not believe her eyes when she saw her employer mowing the lawn.

Nor could Hamish. "Good grief, Owen," he exclaimed. "Your conscience really must have pricked you. What activated it? Seeing this slender young girl doing a man's job?"

Owen stopped and grinned. Kim had never seen him look so human. "I thought I'd nearly give you a heart attack, Hamish. But you're wrong about the conscience. I just couldn't bear to see my housekeeper doing the job so badly."

Hamish glanced at Kim's angry face and said, laughing, "Look out, Owen, your housekeeper will be throwing something at you in a minute. Where are my secateurs? I'd better take hold of them just in case she grabs them and uses them as a missile!"

Owen saw Kim's indignation. "I'm not worried," he drawled. "I can deal with an angry woman, in my own way and," he looked her over lazily, "in my own time."

"Now, now," muttered Hamish to the rose bush he was tending, "any more of that sort of talk, and I shall begin to think you have designs on our Kim. Of the strictly matrimonial variety, of course!"

"And any more of that talk, Hamish," Owen returned snappily, "and I shall begin to think 'our Kim', as you call her, has been taking you into her confidence about her own matrimonial plans – which include me. If she has, she would be running true to form."

Hamish turned idly and looked from one to the other, saw

the tension, felt a fuse had been lit.

Owen went on, "It seems to be an occupational disease of housekeepers, trying to get themselves married to their employers."

Hamish straightened himself, saw Kim's annoyance mounting, and acted fast, stamping out the lighted fuse. "No fear of that in Kim's case." He nodded at her. "With her attractions and her brains, I'm willing to bet some lucky man will snap her up before she's much older, and," he looked hard at Owen, "it won't be you, old chap. You're so slow to appreciate a good thing, even when it's being dangled in front of you like a juicy carrot, she'll be snaffled from under your very nose before you can open your mouth to say 'she's mine'."

Owen went in.

"Sorry about that," Hamish said to Kim, dusting his hands, "but I was only saying something that had to be said." He turned to go, nodding towards the plants he had pruned. "They should be fine now. Any time you want help, just give a call, and I'll be there. So will Daphne." He smiled. "And I'm not just referring to the garden."

As Kim watched him go, depression settled on her like a light covering of snow. Hamish and Daphne were so sane, so level-headed. She knew that life in Owen's house would be impossible without their sympathy and support.

Now her relations with him were back to normal. They were edgy and suspicious of each other. She longed to be his friend, but she could not even be that, let alone anything else. Softly as the fluttering of a moth, the poet's words came back. *"Do you think it so easy to have me become your lover?"* She sighed.

It was too pleasant an evening to go in yet. She breathed in deeply the perfume of the flowers, lustrous and sharply bright in the dying light of evening. She unfolded a garden chair and sat for a while on the concrete near the house, feeling the balm of the air promising summer warmth, listening to the intermittent tranquillising twitter of birdsong.

She heard music and turned to find that Owen was standing at the open french windows and was staring out at the garden, hands in pockets. The sound of the music drifted into the peace and stillness, its beauty stirring, its message deeply moving, and even the birds seemed to revive from their late-evening apathy and join in.

Listening to the harmonies weave and intertwine and resolve into melodious sounds and cadences, Kim felt tears on her cheeks. How much longer, she asked herself, could she go on living in the same house as the man she loved without letting him guess how she felt about him? Without going slowly crazy because, although longing for his touch and his love, she had to keep her distance from him? Without having to remind herself continually that she was his housekeeper and his servant, nothing more?

Yet, even if they had met socially on equal grounds, he, a scientist by conviction as well as career, would have dismissed her with contempt because of her literary background. Their continued acquaintance, even in happier circumstances, would not have stood a chance.

She became aware that the music had stopped. Owen had found himself a chair and was sitting beside her. She rose immediately, thinking she should not be sharing her employer's garden with him, but he put out his hand and pulled her down.

"There's no need for you to go." He looked at her. "Did you like that music, Kim?" He had broken down those barriars again, he had used her name, but she would not, could not respond by doing the same to him.

As he looked, it seemed that even in the dark he could sense there were tears in her eyes.

"It moved you so much?" She nodded, unable to tell him the real cause of her tears. "Did you recognise the music? Do you know the composer?"

"Yes, Mahler. It was his —" She stopped, as she so often had to these days. By her spontaneous recognition of such a modern piece of classical music, she had given herself away again. But she was too tired to be concerned about the questioning look he shot at her. "His —?" Owen prompted.

"The adagietto from his fifth symphony."

"You're quite right." He rose and went in, calling over his shoulder, "See if you recognise this." She heard the music and she did know it. At the end she told him so. "It was a nocturne from Borodin's D-major quartet."

"Full marks." He added quietly, "For a woman with a chosen career such as yours, I find your knowledge of music astounding."

She shivered. She was giving him too many clues. There was a chill in the air and her clothes were inadequate for the lower temperature. He stood immediately and folded his chair, telling her, "Leave yours, I'll see to it. Go in the sitting-room."

It was an order, not an invitation, and it seemed she had to obey. He put the chairs and lawn-mower away in the shed and joined her, closing the french windows behind him. "Sit down, Kim. I'll give you a drink."

"No, thank you." She edged to the door, but he merely repeated, "Sit down," so she obeyed. After all, she was paid to obey him.

He put a glass in her hand and she eyed it with a frown, as though it might be poisonous.

He seemed sensitive to her every reaction. "What's the matter? Don't you like sherry?"

"Yes, yes, of course I do. Thank you." She took a sip. Why was he keeping her there, as though she was a guest and not an employee?

He did not, apparently, seem inclined to talk. He switched on a large standard lamp standing in the corner near the window. It gave just the right amount of light to introduce a subtle intimacy into the atmosphere. He sat down and contemplated his drink in silence, then swallowed it.

"Mr. Lang?" He looked up. "I've often wondered – I know you're a research chemist, but what is your line?"

He laughed and leaned back in his chair, crossing his legs. "So you want to make conversation, do you? You want me to talk about my work, about myself?"

Embarrassed at once, she started to rise. She had obviously overstepped the mark.

"Don't be stupid, girl," he said, "sit down. I wasn't making fun of you. I was just taken aback that a housekeeper of mine was interested enough to want to know how I spend my day. Usually they're here such a short time they hardly learn my surname, let alone my status in life."

She sank down into the armchair, but this time perched on the edge, sitting stiffly.

"For heaven's sake, relax! I can't talk to you if you're determined to look as though you're about to receive a telling off from your employer." He smiled and she returned his smile, forcing herself to relax as he wished her to do. She felt an excitement stirring inside her, but this she immediately bundled into a cupboard in her mind like someone with a precious possession which they took out, gloated over and returned into hiding.

"Anyway," he continued, still smiling, "if you're after me, like all the others, you should be seizing this opportunity I'm giving you, handing you on a plate in fact –"

"So he's testing me," she thought.

"You should seize it with both hands, and make up to me, generally ingratiating yourself with me. You should be using your feminine wiles," he assessed her lazily, eyes half open, "and my word, you have plenty, and inviting me by word and look to make a proposal to you – whether it's moral or immoral makes no difference, it would all lead to the same objective – marriage." Now his smile was cynical. Then softly, "I'm waiting, Kim."

She shook her head, smiling too, but hers was sincere. "I'm not after you, Mr. Lang, I give you my word."

"Pity," he commented easily, "I do so love being elusive to women!" He looked thoughtful. "Now, how do I occupy myself at my place of work? I started off in life as a research chemist. I still am, basically, but with successive promotions I've got progressively farther away from practical research and am now an administrator, a division head. I have a number of scientists under me."

"So you're really in a managerial position?"

"I am. I plan, organise, co-ordinate, interpret results obtained by the scientists working under my direction, and so on. It all adds up to a desk job. As an industrial scientist, and because of the responsible position I hold, I also have to be a kind of salesman, in the sense that I have to communicate the results of the work I am directing to those within the firm who have the money. Over the years, I've acquired the skills of persuasion, case-putting and advocacy, and the higher one gets, the greater the need to do this. My salary is excellent, but I earn it. And, if you're still interested, my line is fibres, man-made."

He leaned forward far enough to be able to touch the trousers she was wearing. He caught a fold of material between his fingers. "I could tell you the name of that material." He nodded at her sleeveless top. "I could, if I thought back to my experimental days, tell you the chemical formula of that material you're wearing." He smiled. "Now I've really got you interested, haven't I?"

"But," she leaned forward now, forgetting her nervousness in her interest in what he was saying, "how on earth do you start to make something that ends up being something that can be cut into with scissors, and sewn and draped and actually worn?"

"Ah, now that's a long, long story. You make fibres by starting with substances that are plainly not fibres but, lo and behold," he moved his hand as if waving a wand, "they cease to be somewhat nasty solids and liquids and become desirable and useful threads. The fibre scientist mixes 'magic' ingredients – in this case, chemicals – and produces something that will in the end become a man-made fibre, like nylon and so on, but which has to be squeezed, pulled, twisted and generally battered about until it takes up a usable form. So the next time you're putting on your beautiful dresses and underwear and what-have-yous, with their delightful feel and their excellent wearing and washing qualities, remember that they all originated in a laboratory and remember to thank the clever scientists who made it possible. Now, having explained about my work and my position, financial and otherwise," he smiled again, "have I made myself attractive enough to make you want to chase after me?"

She crossed her fingers, covering them with her other hand, and hoped the shake of her head was convincing enough to make him believe her. "No," she answered, and surprised herself by the firmness of her tone.

She must have convinced him. His smile was mocking as he drawled, "Pity. By the admiration in your eyes, I really thought I'd made the grade. I must be slipping."

She rose and her smile challenged him. "That was admiration for the scientist's work, not you."

He winced. "That was what might be called a back-hander. You win that point, Kim." He saw her to the door. "The day you can prove to me that your arts graduates, your literary types have made as big a contribution to the material well-being and progress of mankind as scientists have done, I might begin to change my mind about them."

In her heart she agreed with him, so how could she argue against her own beliefs? After all, she came from a family of scientists. She had been the odd one out, the failure, the one who had not been clever enough to make science her career. Then it struck her with some force the expression he had used. She panicked. Had he guessed?

"*My* literary types?"

"Why the sudden anxiety? I merely called them 'yours' because I've noticed you going to their defence whenever I've attacked them."

She began impulsively, "Oh, that's because I'm –" and stopped just in time. She had nearly said, "I'm one myself." As his eyebrows rose, demanding an explanation, she finished feebly, "Sorry, I'm too tired to argue."

"I must remember that in future, and whenever I have any challenging statements to make or," his tone changed and his eyes held a message, "any – er – out-of-the-ordinary demands to make on you, I shall have to wait until you're tired, when you won't have enough energy to argue, then I've a good chance of getting what I want!"

They laughed, exchanged goodnights and parted.

If Kim had thought the friendly relations between them were

to continue, then she was mistaken. Next morning she had a sharp reminder of her subordinate position in the household – her boss was back to normal.

His agreeable mood had gone like a mirage in a desert. Having lowered the barriers to such an extent the previous evening, he must have thought it prudent to remind her in no uncertain terms that he was out of her reach both socially and matrimonially, whatever ideas she might have cherished to the contrary as a result of their pleasant chat the evening before.

At breakfast he was withdrawn, and when he did emerge from behind his newspaper, he was curt. "Remember," he said, "that I'm bringing a colleague home this evening, Miss Paton."

Miss Paton said yes, she hadn't forgotten.

"It won't be a social occasion. We shall be discussing work."

What was the object of that remark? she wondered. To remind her of her lowly place, to tell her in a roundabout way that she was expected to remain in the kitchen the whole evening?

She took Candy to school and got through her work quickly. By early afternoon she had decided to give Owen and his guest steak and mushrooms for the evening meal, plus various tasty additions.

When Candy went into the kitchen after school, she sniffed appreciatively.

"Your daddy's having a guest to dinner, Candy," Kim said. "They'll be talking business most of the time, so you must be very quiet while they have their meal."

"Can't I have it in the kitchen with you?"

"My goodness," said Kim, "I don't think your daddy would like that."

"Why not? I wish I could have it with you every evening. It would be much more fun than having it with Daddy. He never talks to me."

Kim thought it advisable to change the subject. "I'm going to make pastry, Candy. Like to help?"

There was nothing Candy liked better and it kept her occupied until Kim went upstairs to wash and change. She thought she should make herself look agreeable since there was a visitor coming. She discarded her slacks and found a trim navy pinafore dress amongst her clothes, which she teamed with a white polo-necked sweater. She looked neat and efficient and the navy belt at her waist revealed a shapeliness which could not easily be overlooked.

As soon as Owen opened the front door and showed his guest into the house, Candy called out, "Daddy, I want to have my tea with Kim, not you."

Kim had not dared to emerge from the kitchen. Candy could have put it more tactfully, she thought. But the answer was reasonable.

"Good idea, Candy. Where's Miss Paton?"

Miss Paton made her appearance and saw her employer's guest. He was shorter than Owen, thick-set, with a face that would have been handsome had his way of living not begun to deprive him of his looks. He had the appearance of one who had made a fetish of self-indulgence and who was willing to pay the price of his pleasure-seeking habits.

Owen introduced them. "Miss Paton – my colleague, Marvin Ward."

The fingers which the man extended towards her were brown-stained with nicotine, his eyes which darted over her held a sensuality which was unmistakable and his overall plumpness proclaimed the preoccupation with food of a gourmet.

As he moved with his host into the sitting-room, Kim heard him say in a voice which he did not bother to lower, "You sly devil, Owen, you didn't tell me you had a miniature Venus in the house. Who is she?"

"I told you, my housekeeper."

Owen's colleague laughed unbelievingly. "Come off it, boy. Your woman, more likely. There's no need to pretend with me."

Kim retreated to the kitchen, hearing her employer's voice assure his guest that Miss Paton was his housekeeper pure and simple, adding "and I mean pure and simple."

As Kim served the meal, Marvin Ward watched every movement she made. Owen, on the other hand, ignored her and continued the technical discussion all the time she was in the room. As she poured out their coffee, Marvin Ward said to her, in the mood of one making an experiment and wondering what the result would be,

"I compliment you on your efficiency, Miss Paton. Had a lot of experience in this line?"

She knew his aim was to make her talk, nothing else, so she answered vaguely, "A certain amount, Mr. Ward."

He seemed to like the sound of her voice and had obviously decided instantly in which category to place her. Now his expression revealed the course of his thoughts. A new object to pursue, he seemed to have decided, a personality he could not quite pin down and one, therefore, that intrigued him.

He caught her hand as she passed him. "Ever have any free time?"

Kim coloured and pulled her hand away. This apparently intrigued the man even more.

Owen growled, "Will you leave us, Miss Paton? We were in the middle of an important discussion when you interrupted us."

Kim swallowed the retort she would dearly loved to have given and went out, hearing Marvin Ward say, "How can you talk to such a luscious creature like that? As interesting a piece of femininity as it's ever been my luck to meet."

"Keep your mauling hands off that girl, Marvin," Owen replied, his voice coming through the closed door. "I'm warning you."

Kim was so flushed by the time she reached the kitchen, Candy asked her if she was hot. Yes, Kim thought, hot with anger and embarrassment. Who did Owen Lang think she was — some impressionable, ingenuous little Victorian parlour-maid?

When Marvin Ward was leaving, he pushed open the kitchen door and thanked Kim for cooking such a delicious meal. Owen stood stiffly behind him, apparently impatient for his guest to be gone. But Marvin Ward seemed impervious to his host's displeasure.

"We'll meet again some time, Miss Paton?" Marvin asked "I'll ring you, how's that?"

Kim's eyes moved to Owen's and saw the anger there.

"Well, Mr. Ward," she replied, "I – perhaps . . ."

The hope in his eyes grew into anticipation. She guessed how his mind was working and knew then that her answer should have been a downright refusal. This was a man to be wary of.

But something, some perversity, provoked by her employer's open disapproval, stopped her from turning Marvin Ward down flat.

He took her hesitation for encouragement. "Right." He raised his hand. "Will do."

Owen caught her as she was about to go to bed. "I'm warning you off my colleague, Miss Paton. He already has a string of women friends and is notorious for discarding them one after the other – after the event. And, in case you happen to be interested, he never marries them."

She faced him resolutely. "Thank you for your advice, and also for your touchingly paternal interest in my love-life, Mr. Lang. I appreciate it, even if it does make you sound like a Victorian master of the house telling his servant-girl she's not allowed to have any 'followers' " she watched his eyes harden, "but it's very doubtful whether I shall require such fatherly advice. Few men keep their promises, and Mr. Ward's statement that he will contact me was not even a promise. Goodnight, Mr. Lang."

He caught her arm as she began to climb the stairs. "But if he does try to date you, will you go out with him?"

She rebelled, resentful that he should take it upon himself to interfere in her private life. "I really don't know, Mr. Lang." She made her voice bored. "It depends on what – er – mood I'm in at the time he rings." Half-way up the stairs she turned. "In any case, it's my business entirely. I'm your employee, not your slave. Goodnight, Mr. Lang."

She turned her back on his fury and went to bed.

Kim was on her knees weeding the flower-beds the following afternoon when the telephone brought her flying into the house. It was Marvin Ward. He had obviously decided to waste no time. He invited her to dine with him that evening.

She recalled her employer's authoritarian attitude over Marvin Ward's interest in her and, defiance welling up like the waters of a fountain, she accepted Marvin's invitation.

When Owen arrived home she asked for the evening off. "I've had no proper free time since I came," she reminded him, but even her reminder seemed to irritate him. "I haven't asked for it because I haven't particularly wanted it, but –"

"I'm well aware of that and was going to mention it. So you're going out with Marvin Ward, despite what I told you about his reputation?" She nodded. "Yes, I see now." His eyes narrowed. "A bit of bad psychology on my part. It probably made you keener than ever to go out with him, rake that he is, or, as you would probably call him in your hypocritical, ladylike language, man of the world."

"How did you know I was going out with him?"

"He told me this afternoon. Don't forget I'm his division head. He said he'd rung you and you had accepted. He said," and Owen looked at her with something like disgust, "that you had 'jumped at the chance of going out with him.' He informed me that he was looking forward to a very – profitable evening. He also said something else. If I tell you, it might make you cry off. On the other hand, it might make you even more determined. I'll be interested to see your reaction. He said, 'I'm going to get that girl by fair means or foul! I assume you know what he meant?"

She did not answer him directly. "Thank you again," she said, "for your kindly interest in my moral welfare, but I was not born yesterday. I'm not unfamiliar with the ways of men."

"No, I'm sure you're not! I'm aware of the fact that you have a string of boy-friends at home. But what about the 'special' one – John, isn't it?"

She shrugged with what she hoped was convincing nonchalance.

He went on, "Out of sight, out of mind, eh? Women make

me sick. They're such loyal creatures to their men! I've suffered in the past from women like you." She knew he was referring to his late wife. "You're the sort, aren't you, who likes an assortment of men-friends – a different one to entertain each evening."

She shrugged again. If he liked to think that of her, she wouldn't trouble to disenchant him. "Mr. Lang, I may be an ignorant, untutored housekeeper, but I know how to manage men."

"There are, to my knowledge, Miss Paton, only two ways for a woman to 'manage' a man, as you call it. Either she says 'no' or she says 'yes'. Which do you choose?"

"That's my business."

He plainly took that statement the wrong way. "I have my own way of describing women like you, and it's very uncomplimentary!" She avoided his eyes. "All right, go out with him. I'm sure you, too, will have a – 'profitable' evening. I don't somehow think you'll let all that –" he looked her over insultingly, "magnetism go to waste."

She said levelly, "I'll get your meal, Mr. Lang."

That night, when Kim put Candy to bed, she told her she was going out. Candy clung tightly. "Who with – my daddy?"

Kim saw the odd light of hope in the blue eyes.

"No, darling. Someone else."

The light in the eyes went out. "Do you mean that man who came last night? No, don't go out with him." Her hold tightened. "I don't like him."

"There's nothing wrong with him, Candy."

"There is!"

"But we're only going to have something to eat somewhere, then I'll come home."

"Promise?" Candy whispered. "Promise you'll come home?"

Kim had to fight the tears. "Of course I'll come home, Candy."

"Home", she had said. And for the moment she had meant it. But, she had to remind herself severely, it was not her home. It was her place of work, no more, no less. She hushed the

longing which awoke inside her, like a mother soothing a sob-
bing baby.

But Candy had not finished with her. "Kim," she pulled
her down and whispered in her ear, "why are you and my
daddy always quarrelling?"

"Candy darling –" but the words caught in her throat. What
answer could she give which would provide the child with the
reassurance, the security she sought?

"Don't you like my daddy?" Candy persisted.

"Of course I do, but –"

"Doesn't he like you?"

"I – I don't know, Candy. I don't – think – he does."

"But why not?" Her hold became strangling. "I like you.
I love you."

Kim kissed her forehead and held her tightly, then slipped
out of the room before Candy could see the tears in her eyes.

When Marvin called for her, Owen was nowhere to be seen.
Kim was glad. She could not have stood his look of contempt.

Marvin, however, was appreciative, volubly so. He commented on her taste in clothes – she was wearing a white lacy
top and a well-fitting deep red skirt. She had put on her make-
up with care and brushed her hair until it crackled. It was her
first evening out for weeks, so why shouldn't she look her best?

The hungry look in Marvin's eyes held a foretaste of what
he was certain would be coming his way later. They dined
against a background of subdued lighting and soft, sentimental
music. As they ate, they talked, about Marvin's work as a
"back-room boy" – "Boffins we used to be called, years ago
– still are, sometimes." His hours, he said, were irregular, no
nine-to-five job for him.

"If we get on to something in the lab. we have to see it
through. We can't get away as if we had a desk job, like Owen.
We have time off, though, when the others are at work. I like
it that way. It fits in better with my plans, my –" he eyed
her, gauging her reaction, "my private life."

She was silent, concentrating on her meal.

"You've heard, I suppose," he went on, "about the multitude of women friends I'm alleged to have?"

"Yes. From Mr. Lang." She smiled. "I suppose you're going to deny every word."

"I'm certainly not. It's true, and the women are true, every single one of them." He lifted his fingers to start counting, but Kim broke in,

"I also have it from Mr. Lang that you have every intention of making me one of them."

"Quite right. I like the way you come straight to the point. No hypocrisy. Any objections if I do?"

"Plenty. I'm not that sort. Just thought I'd let you know at the start."

He smiled knowingly. "That's what they all say – at first."

She started to rise indignantly, but he pulled her back.

"Now now, no offence." He grinned confidently. "You'll just take me a little longer, that's all. I thrive on opposition. It sharpens my appetite. All the more fun when I eventually win."

She was nettled and showed it. He patted her hand. "Forget it – for the moment."

They found a place to dance and he held her as if they were intimate friends. She objected strongly, but kept her emotions under control, knowing he would interpret resistance as an open invitation to proceed.

The evening passed pleasantly and Marvin proved good company. It was on the way home in the car that Kim first became worried. He stopped without warning in a side-road and pulled her across to kiss him. She went rigid and unyielding. He did not seem put out and tried again. Her response was the same.

To her infinite relief he thought better of it and let her go. Whether it was her determined resistance to his approaches, or whether he had in mind the fact that her employer was his immediate boss at work, she would never know, but she slumped thankfully away from him and sat silent for the rest of the journey.

As he drew up outside Owen's house, he said, holding her hand, "I've heard a saying which claims that 'the difficult takes time, the impossible a little longer.' You, sweetie, will just take a 'little longer'."

She shook her head, laughing, but in her heart she knew she was playing with fire.

CHAPTER VII

"You were late in last night, Miss Paton." Her employer greeted her sourly as he took his place at the breakfast table.

"I'm sorry if I disturbed you."

"You didn't disturb me. I hadn't gone to bed."

This angered her. "There was no need to wait up for me like an over-anxious parent. I'm not a child."

His eyes rested on her face and narrowed in their scrutiny. "I'm sure you're not – now."

She knew what he was implying, but did not deny his silent accusation. Let him think what he liked!

Candy came bounding in and flung her arms round Kim's waist. "You came home, Kim, you promised, and you came home!"

"But, darling," Kim bent and touched Candy's cheek with her lips, "of course I came home."

"Daddy said," Candy seized the milk jug and swamped her cereal with the contents, "you might stay out all night."

Kim swung round, white with anger. "How *could* you?"

His smile mocked her protest. "It was on the cards, Miss Paton, knowing, as I do, the persuasive technique of my colleague."

"I've told you before, Mr. Lang, I was not born yesterday. I don't succumb to 'persuasive techniques.'"

"Of course," came softly, derisively, "you know how to handle men, you said. You know how to say 'no' – and 'yes'." He rubbed his chin speculatively. "Now I wonder what your answer was?"

His question remained unanswered.

It was not until later, when Kim was on her way to collect Candy from school, that it came to her with a shock that it was only two days to her birthday. It was something she had to keep to herself at all costs, otherwise awkward questions

114

would be asked. Owen would assume she had reached the age of thirty. Candy would want to know too much. She would demand "celebrations" and would insist on giving her a present.

It *would* have to be a Saturday! Kim set her alarm for a quarter of an hour before the postman's usual time of arrival, planning to creep downstairs and gather all the cards she knew her family would send her. She would carry them up to her room and hide them away until it was safe to take them out and look at them.

But she had reckoned without the odd quirk of fate. That morning the postman was early. He rang the bell loudly and insistently, anxious to deliver his bundles and be on his way.

Kim dived for her dressing-gown, tying it round her waist as she ran down the stairs. Candy was close behind, excited by all the noise the postman was making.

Kim unbolted the front door and took the armful of cards and presents. Now she could hide nothing. Candy was dancing up and down with delight. "Who are they for? For you? For Daddy?"

No point now in trying to conceal the truth. "For me, Candy. It's my birthday."

That set Candy racing up the stairs to hammer on her father's door. "Wake up, get up, Daddy! It's Kim's birthday!"

Fortunately for Kim, Candy's father seemed reluctant to leave his bed at such an unearthly hour on a Saturday morning. There was a muffled groan and a ruffling of bedclothes, then silence.

Kim sat on her bed with Candy wriggling beside her and opened her cards. She went slowly through the pile – her friends and relatives must have got her address from her mother – and came to her parents' card. Its loving message brought tears to her eyes and a feeling of nostalgia for her home surroundings.

It was her brother's card which gave her a shock. His, of course, was "different". He had bought two children's cards – one for a two-year-old with a large "2" on it, and one for a four-year-old, bearing a large "4". He had stuck them together so that the number 24 was there before her, bold and unmistakable, followed by a jumble of childish greetings.

Candy thought it was wonderful. "Your brother doesn't know how old you are!" she chortled. "He thinks you're two or four. That makes you younger than me!" She hugged Kim delightedly.

Kim, far from delighted, slid her brother's creation under the pile of envelopes and hoped it would be quietly forgotten.

Then came the presents. Her parents had sent her a warm, expensive-looking cardigan with the message, "For our cold English summer." Various aunts and cousins had given her perfume, talc, handkerchiefs and gloves.

But it was her brother again who made her scarlet with embarrassment. His gift was a short transparent nightdress in deep pink and trimmed with black. The message ran, "Happy dreams. One of my girl-friends chose it!" In brackets were the words, "If you're wearing this when there's a man around, especially you-know-who, remember Newton's first law of motion."

"What does that mean?" asked Candy.

"I don't know, but I wish I did," Kim muttered.

She went to the mirror and held the nightdress against her. Candy squealed with rapture.

There came a voice from the door, "Aren't you going to try it on, Miss Paton?"

She swung round, the nightdress still against her, and saw her employer's mocking smile. He was leaning against the bedroom door, hands in his dressing-gown pockets. "Who gave you that?" he asked. "One of your – hopeful – boy-friends?"

"No." She turned back to the mirror. "My brother."

"*What?* Do you mean he went into a shop and –?"

"No. One of his girl-friends chose it."

"*One* of his girl-friends? Of course, you told me he has a number."

"A large number."

"It runs in the family, doesn't it? Lovers galore."

She said airily, "Oh, he's much worse than I am."

"Daddy," said Candy, rummaging among the cards and

116

paper on the bed, "what's a law of motion?" She found the piece of paper she was looking for and held it out to him.

"A what?" asked her startled father.

Kim dived to catch the paper as it passed from daughter to father, but it reached its destination — Owen's hand — a fraction of a second before she could intervene. Even so, she tried to snatch it from him, but he caught her wrist with one hand and with the other held the paper high in the air.

"Please, Mr. Lang," she pleaded, "*please* give it to me." On no account could he be allowed to read it.

"Certainly, Miss Paton," he was still holding her, "when I've finished with it." His eyebrows shot up, then he threw back his head and laughed. "I like that," he said, releasing her and handing the paper back to her. "I really like that. Yes, I know Newton's first law of motion."

"Tell us," urged Candy. But her father refused. Instead he changed the subject.

"Your brother, Miss Paton — he's scientifically inclined?"

The way he phrased the question gave her an escape route. With luck she would be able to avoid telling him the whole truth.

"Yes, he is." She could see Owen was waiting for more, but Candy provided a welcome diversion. She pulled Kim down on to the bed beside her.

"Come on, Daddy, sit next to me and look at Kim's cards and presents."

Owen did as he was told and Kim, acutely embarrassed, passed them across to him. He admired them all, and if he was puzzled by the amount they must have cost — their quality showed — he said nothing about it.

Candy got up. "Sit here, Daddy." She put her hands on his shoulders and tried in vain to shift his bulk along the bed to occupy her place. When he did not oblige, her voice rose to a note of appeal. "Move *along*, Daddy, sit next to Kim, Daddy."

Slowly and with seeming reluctance, he complied. Candy surveyed them happily. "Now I'm going to look for a present for Kim."

"Candy, no, darling. It doesn't matter . . ." But Candy had

117

gone, and Kim was alone with Owen.

"I'm sorry about this," she said at last. He did not respond. "But it's easy to see what she's trying to do, isn't it?"

"Yes, it is, Miss Paton." He was staring at the floor. "I can read Candy's mind. She is, after all, my own daughter. She's – trying to bring us together."

He walked to the window and stared out. "But, like an obstinate fish whose appetite has been satiated as a result of eating its fill in the past," she knew he was referring to his unsatisfactory marriage, "I refuse to bite." He half-turned and looked at her. "Tempting though the bait may be." He had caught her unawares and she had not had time to hide the unhappiness in her eyes. "Disappointed, Miss Paton?"

"You know the answer to that, Mr. Lang. You also know my views on scientists."

"Ah, yes. I remember what you said at the Souths' that evening. You wouldn't marry one for a fortune. But you're getting a bit old to be so choosey, aren't you? Thirty years old today?"

"*Thirty?*" She corrected herself hastily. "Oh yes, thirty."

Candy returned holding something wrapped in tissue. "Daddy! *Daddy!* You moved. You moved away from Kim." She caught his arm and pulled him back to sit on the bed beside his housekeeper. Then she handed over Kim's present.

With slow questing fingers, Kim removed the wrapping and found what she had been dreading – an object so precious it almost amounted to a sacrificial offering. It was a doll dressed in crinoline-style costume. The skirt was a stiff white material with an overskirt of delicate, shining pink. The bodice was square-necked with full sleeves and the long hair was gold with a headband of tiny pink roses. The eyes opened and shut and the arms moved.

It was in perfect, cherished condition. "But, Candy," Kim protested, tears in her eyes, "darling, this is yours. You mustn't give it to me –"

"It's yours now. It's your birthday present from me."

A voice said quietly beside her, "It's her most precious possession, Miss Paton. You must accept it, I'm afraid. She means it."

Kim shook her head, unable to speak. Then she stood and put her arms round Candy, pressing her cheek to the little girl's soft one.

"My cheek's wet," said Candy, feeling it. "Why are you crying, Kim?" Kim could not answer. "Why is she crying, Daddy?" Candy sounded anxious.

Her father answered, "Because she likes her present so much, Candy. Isn't that true, Kim?"

Kim nodded. Silently the father handed her his handkerchief. Kim dried her eyes and said she would wash the handkrchief and return it, but he took it from her and stuffed it into his dressing-gown pocket.

"Now your present, Daddy."

Owen looked nonplussed. He stood up, disconcerted. "I haven't got one." He looked down at Kim, quite at a loss. "How could I, when I didn't even know?"

"No, no, thank you. I've got enough presents." She looked at him. "*You* can't give me one." Her tone sounded belligerent, although she had not meant it to be.

"Can't I?" His voice sounded odd, as though she had challenged him. "We'll have to see, won't we?"

Candy, sitting again beside Kim, jumped up and down in her excitement. "Yes, we will." As she moved, she dislodged the pile of birthday cards and they slid to the floor. The card Kim had tried so hard to conceal was lying on the carpet at Owen's feet, staring him in the face.

He bent down and picked it up. He looked at the figures, the "two" and the "four".

"My — my brother's little joke," she explained, trying to pass it off.

She looked up fearfully. Would he be angry? Surprised? Indignant?

He was smiling as though he had expected it. "Twenty-four," he murmured. "Not twenty-nine, not thirty, but twenty-four. When I privately assessed your age as twenty-three, I wasn't far wrong, was I?" He dropped the card on to the bed. "Another veil, Miss Paton? Another lie? And more to come, no doubt?"

She picked up the doll Candy had given her and stroked its hair. "Do you want me to leave, Mr. Lang," she whispered, "because I'm too young for the job?"

Silence greeted her question and she was afraid to look up and see the dismissal in his eyes. At last the answer came. "What do you really expect me to say to that, Kim?" She looked at him forlornly. "Yes, go now, this minute? Is that what you want me to say? And on your birthday, too?"

She shook her head, her eyes appealing.

"Then I won't say it. Not now."

There was a sigh of relief beside them. Kim realised that Candy had been listening and all was well in her world again. But as Kim watched them go, the two words he had just spoken hung upon the air like poisonous exhaust fumes. "Not now," he had said, ominously, warning her, like a threat. "Not now," he had meant, "but all in good time, when it suits me."

After breakfast, Candy demanded loudly and insistently that they should do "something special" because it was Kim's birthday. "Let's go out somewhere."

"What do you suggest?" asked her father, not unwilling to agree to her request. "Tea in the country? Dinner out this evening?"

Candy supplied the answer. "A picnic. By the lake in the woods."

Owen murmured, his eyes glinting, "A sort of family outing, eh, Miss Paton?"

But she refused to be goaded into retaliating on her birthday. After lunch, while Kim prepared the sandwiches, Candy dragged her father to the shops. "To get your present from Daddy," she explained, and there was no arguing with her.

By the time they returned, the food and drink were ready and waiting in a hold-all. Owen called his housekeeper into the sitting-room. "I've been instructed to perform the presentation ceremony with the pomp and flourish which the occasion demands." He handed over a long, narrow box and as Kim unwrapped it, her heart pounded unmercifully.

Inside was a gold chain bracelet lying in a black velvetined bed. It was secured about the wrist by a miniature gold padlock. It must have cost a large sum of money. Her eyes thanked him, yet reproached him. "There was no need, Mr. Lang, but thank you *very* much."

"Candy chose it," he said, "and who was I to argue?"

Kim tried to fasten it round her wrist, but fumbled. "May I?" Owen clipped the bracelet into place, the touch of his fingers caressing in her skin.

"Aren't you going to kiss him?" Candy demanded, watching them anxiously. "Like you kissed me, Kim?"

"Now," his eyes twinkled, "my daughter has something here, Miss Paton." He waited while she searched his face to see if he was serious. "Come on," he was impatient now, "it's your birthday, so to hell with convention." He bent down.

Shyly she reached up to kiss his cheek, but his hand jerked up and clamped on to her face. He turned it towards him and kissed her lips. Slowly, holding her eyes, he released her. Breathlessly, pulsatingly, she drew away.

Candy clapped her hands. She was alight with joy, convinced beyond all doubt that her ruse, innocent and almost unconscious though it was, was working.

The lake was a calm stretch of water in the centre of a wood. The afternoon was close and the sun appeared at frequent intervals, if somewhat coyly, from behind the clouds. The blackberry bushes, keeping the magnitude of their autumn crop a close secret, smelled sweet in the spring air.

They had their tea under the trees, Candy sitting in the centre, feeding the birds with the crusts which she tore off her sandwiches. She asked permission to paddle, removed her sandals and ran to stand in the gently lapping water at the edge of the lake.

Owen watched her for a while, then lay back, his arms across his eyes. Kim, a foot or two away, followed his example. They lay, listening to the birdsong and buzz of the insects, saying nothing. The words of the poet drifted into Kim's mind.

121

"For the one I love most lay sleeping by me
under the same cover in the cool night."

She stirred uneasily and he responded by turning his head.

"I'm sorry to force my company on you, Miss Paton, especially on your birthday. You could have been so much better occupied, couldn't you? Out on a date, perhaps, with Marvin Ward?"

She resisted the temptation to answer his sarcasm. Instead she said, "I know you came to please Candy, not me, Mr Lang. So did I."

He lay still, his eyes closed. She turned her head towards him. "Mr. Lang?" He murmured in answer. "I think we both know what Candy is desperately trying to do." Still no reply. "Mr. Lang, she needs a mother, a real mother, not just a housekeeper taking the place of one."

"You wouldn't, by any chance, be proposing to me, Miss Paton?" He had not moved, but his words pained her like a bite inflicted by a vicious animal.

"Always," she ground out, tears lurking in her voice, "always you come back to the same thing, the same place, like someone lost in a forest going round in circles. What can I do to convince you I haven't got you in my matrimonial sights? I'm not getting married for years. I have my life in front of me, my career to follow . . ." She stopped, dismayed.

But he was on to it. His head shot round. "Career? What career?"

How could she explain her statement without arousing his suspicions? "My — my career as a housekeeper."

He shouted with laughter and the noise drifted away over the tree-tops. "And what a career! Devoting your life to running round after irritable, bad-tempered, impossible men like me."

She repeated quietly, "Candy needs a mother, Mr. Lang. You owe it to her. You can't go on for ever fobbing her off with second-best, with someone you have to *pay* to look after her. You can pay for attention, but you can't pay for love, real love."

He raised himself on his elbow, his eyes raking her from head to foot. "Can't you, Miss Paton, can't you?"

She met his eyes. "You're deliberately misunderstanding me. I'm talking about mother-love, not — not —"

He supplied the word she was too shy to use. "Lust?"

She turned her head away. He became thoughtful, pulling at the grass between them. "Do you know, Miss Paton, I might take your advice. I'll find my daughter a mother."

She took a tight hold of herself. She would not let even the trace of a tear betray her feelings. "That's good," she blurted out, "then you can dismiss me with impunity, you can get me out of your hair."

He shifted nearer, hovering over her. "You know damned well I can't dismiss you, don't you?"

She looked at him, confused to find how near he was. "Because of Candy?"

"Because of —" Without warning his head came down, his lips fastened on hers and his arms gathered her to him. So shocked was she that she allowed his kiss to go on and on, rejoicing in it even — until she was sickened by a thought that sidled into her mind. "You can pay for love," he had asserted. He was testing her, trying her out, preparing the ground for future cultivation. Perhaps when they got home he might even suggest . . .

She struggled violently and freed herself, her face scarlet, her hair awry. He dropped back into his original position, lying full length, his hand over his eyes. His breathing was heavy, but otherwise he showed no unusual sign of disturbance or agitation.

Do you think it so easy to have me become your lover? She scrambled up and ran, ran away from him to his daughter, who was laughing at the ducklings as they trailed, follow-my-leader, after their mother.

That evening, Marvin phoned. Owen took the call and handed the receiver to her, his face stone cold. Marvin asked, would she go out with him the next evening she was free? Why not? she thought. She was surely entitled to a little pleasure now and then.

"Yes, I'd like to, Marvin." They arranged a date and tim He said he would look forward to it with anticipation an pleasure.

Before she went to bed, she thanked Owen again for h present.

"Don't thank me," he said, without looking at her, "it wa Candy's idea, not mine."

At breakfast next morning, Owen retreated as usual behin his newspaper. Before Candy came down, Kim dared to di turb him, to tear down that barrier of newsprint.

"Mr. Lang?" He lowered the newspaper irritably. "Woul you have any objection if next weekend I went home to se my parents?" She looked down. "I miss them rather, and –"

He gave his permission and asked when she would be going.

"Friday afternoon, if you don't mind, after collectin Candy from school. Daphne would have her until you g home."

"You intend staying away two nights? Go ahead. I dare say I can manage without a housekeeper for a couple of day: I'm not helpless."

She said hesitantly, "You can deduct it from my salary if you want . . ."

"Don't be so damned stupid," was his acid comment as h left for work.

She went out with Marvin. They saw a play and had a lat supper at a restaurant. He said, "What I can't fathom is ho\ an intelligent girl like you can tackle a mundane job lik housekeeping. You've been educated – that sticks out a mile What happened to bring you down to this level?"

Incautious with tiredness, made unusually articulate an trusting by the lateness of the hour, she told him she had degree but in a subject so useless she couldn't get herself job.

"There are so many graduates like me around, graduate in subjects that have little application to present-day need: that competition for any jobs that are going is frightening

Since I couldn't face teaching as a career, and nobody else wanted me working for them, here I am. But," she put her finger to her lips like a drunken person – she was drunk, with fatigue, not alcohol – "don't whatever you do tell Owen. He'd throw me out on the spot, if he knew. If there's one thing he can't stand, he says, won't have in his house, in fact, it's an arts graduate. So you see why I'm keeping quiet about it."

"Is that so?" A calculating look sneaked into his eyes and it came to Kim, through the veils of tiredness, that something was wrong. She had trusted the man, and her trust had been misplaced.

"You won't tell Owen, Marvin? Promise you won't tell?"

"Now," he took her hand, "that depends, darling." He looked at his watch. "Time we were going."

In the car, his hand felt for hers. She snatched it away. So he patted her knee and she moved that. He pulled up in a country lane and she tried to get out, but she knew it was futile even to try.

"Behave," he said, "and just do what I want. I won't hurt you."

He tried to kiss her, but she twisted away.

"I'm not coming out with you again. You obviously haven't got the message, I'm not that sort. And I mean it!"

He took his hands away and shrugged. "There's plenty of time," he said. "You'll come round." He drove on. "Easy does it. You'll give in. I never force the pace. Willing surrender is so much easier on the nerves than attempted rape. I always win in the end. And what's more, my sweet, I've got a hold over you, haven't I?"

"What do you mean?"

"If you don't come out with me, I'll tell Owen everything. It's as simple as that. I see him at work every day, don't I?"

She muttered, "Owen said you were not to be trusted. I wish I'd listened to him."

" 'Owen' is it, now? How far has he got with you, I wonder? Are you in love with him yet?" He looked at her sharply. "Yes, I think you are. I could tell him that, too."

"You," she said through her teeth, "are the most unscru
pulous –'

"Fair means or foul," he laughed, "I said I'd get you."

He pulled up outside Owen's house and under a street lamp
He grabbed her before she could get out, and gave her a pas
sionate kiss. She hurled herself out of the car. As she ran up
the garden path she saw to her dismay the curtain in Owen'
sitting-room being lowered into place. He must have seen Mar
vin kissing her.

Kim drove herself to her parents' home on Friday afternoon
her happy anticipation at being reunited with her family tem
pered with sadness when she remembered Candy's farewell.

Candy had clung to her as if she would never let her go
"You'll come back, Kim, promise you'll come back," she ha
said.

Daphne's eyes had been full of compassion as she watched
Kim disentangle herself from the small gripping arms.

"All my things will still be here, Candy," Kim had tried
to reassure her. "Of course I'll be back." She had crouched
down to the child's height. "How would you like it, Candy, i'
I phoned you tomorrow?"

Candy had wanted to know the time to the very minute
when the promised phone call would come.

Now Kim's arms were clasping her mother like Candy's
had clung to her. "It's nice to be back, Mum," Kim said, a
little girl again for a few seconds.

"Lovely to see you, darling." She had hugged her daughter,
then inspected her closely. "You look well, although you must
have worked hard.'

"It's not so much the work, it's the emotional undercur-
rents that get me. It's so wearing."

"Is Mr. Lang difficult, dear?"

"Difficult? He's impossible. But at other times ..." She
shook her head, averting her eyes to keep her secret to herself.

Her father kissed her chek and asked, was it the house she
was keeping, or its occupants? Then he wandered into the
dining-room while the women talked, and started to set the

126

table. Kim watched him with tears of thankfulness that her parents and their ways had not changed at all while she had been away.

Perry swept in for his meal with a typical Perry-like question. He eyed her up and down and asked bluntly, "What, still virginal? Good heavens, either you must have learnt really effective evasive tactics – or the man isn't normal."

His sister snorted, "He's normal all right."

Perry looked at her keenly. "So it's you being clever, is it? Hold him off, dear sister, that's the way to keep a man eager. Take a tip from your big brother."

"Be quiet, Perry," his mother reprimanded her son mildly. She had long ago abandoned her efforts to reform him. "Stop trying to make Kim as dissolute as you are."

Over dinner, Perry told her he was on the trail of a job that might interest her. "One of my friends has a contact who's looking for a girl to join a television production team to work on documentary programmes. He wants an English graduate because there's some background research involved. Right up your street," he commented, between mouthfuls. "You'd be a fool not to consider it."

"Much better use of your university training, dear," her father commented, "than making beds and washing floors."

At first the idea excited Kim. It was a job in a thousand and she would be using her intellect which had somehow gone to sleep on her in the past few weeks. "Is there time to think it over, Perry? He doesn't want an answer straight away?"

"Good heavens," Perry said, "why the hesitation? Don't tell me you want to go on housekeeping?"

"Of course I don't," Kim snapped, thrown off balance by her own indecision, "but –" She felt again Candy's arms clinging to her neck, heard her whisper, "You *will* come back, won't you?" "I just can't explain, Perry. You wouldn't understand." She looked dubiously at her mother. "Mum might."

After the meal, Perry left. He patted his sister's head. "You take that job, Kim. Cut loose from that profligate scientist." He raised his hand to his family and grinned. "Ah well, back to nature." He went out.

127

Later, Kim phoned all her boy-friends in turn and chatted for nearly an hour. When she rang off, she told her mother of her dilemma, about her job, but her mother had no answer, no solution to offer.

"It's something you'll have to work out for yourself, Kim. I feel for that poor little child, but it's up to her father, isn't it, to solve his own problems."

"But you don't know Candy, Mum. She's such a good little soul. I wish I could have brought her with me."

Her mother looked concerned. "Darling, you must *not* get too fond of her. It wouldn't do at all, would it? You'll have to leave there one day, and as far as I can judge, the sooner the better, the way things are going."

She did not tell her mother about her other problem – her love for Owen. That was something too precious to discuss with anyone, even her own mother.

The following evening at exactly the time she had arranged, Kim phoned Candy. Owen answered. He was abrupt but not surprised. He had obviously expected the call. No doubt Candy had waited all day for it. At last Candy spoke, and found hardly anything to say.

Kim was so moved to hear her voice, she ran dry, too. She looked at her own mother standing beside her.

"Candy," said Kim, "my mummy is here with me. Would you like to speak to her? You would?"

Her mother shook her head and whispered, "Now you're getting me involved, you naughty girl!" Then, into the telephone, "Is that you, Candy? This is Kim's mother here. How are you, Candy?" Her mother listened. "Yes, I expect you are missing Kim. Yes, don't worry," she made a face at her daughter, "yes, Kim will be coming back. Do you like school, Candy? What, you play the recorder? You clever girl! Kim could never play anything when she was little. You like writing stories? Do you, darling? You write lots of stories? You must let Kim read them some time. Oh, I see, you write them at school. I'm so glad to have spoken to you, Candy. You want to speak to Kim again?"

The receiver was handed over. "Yes, Candy," Kim said,

"I'm coming back. No, not tonight, tomorrow. Tomorrow evening. Yes, darling, I promise. Goodnight, Candy."

As she replaced the phone, Kim's eyes filled with tears. "What can I do, Mum?"

"Darling," said her mother, "I don't know. I just don't know."

On the day of her return, Kim was late getting away. All her boy-friends had called and Perry had brought a girl-friend and there was a minor party.

Kim promised her mother, as they embraced before she left, to think seriously about the job Perry had mentioned. She would love to take it, she said, if only . . . Her mother said she understood. "But you've got your own life to lead, Kim. You can't be tied for ever to someone else's child, darling though she is."

The journey back took much longer than Kim anticipated. She had to make a diversion into a town to get some petrol, as so many filling stations on the way were closed.

She was tired and she was hungry and she arrived back to chaos. Owen greeted her on the doorstep, white-faced and angry. Where had she been? Why was she so late? Candy had nearly driven him mad saying Kim was not coming back.

"She's been screaming the place down," he said. "I had to have Daphne in to calm her down, but even then she wouldn't stop crying."

"But, Mr. Lang, I was delayed. First, my friends came unexpectedly –"

"Your *friends*? Are they more important than your job?"

Now she was white-faced, with fatigue and misery. "You're being quite unfair, Mr. Lang. I promised Candy I would come back –"

"So did all the others. When it got so late, she thought you had broken your promise, like all the others."

"Where is she now?"

"With Daphne. I'll go and get her."

But there was no need. They had seen her car in the sideway. A little pyjama-clad figure came flying through the front door and straight into Kim's waiting arms. Again the child clung, tighter than ever before, and Kim swung her in her arms and held her shaking shivering form as a mother does a beloved child.

"I thought you weren't coming back," Candy sobbed.

"But, Candy," Kim said, her voice urgent, "I promised." It was no use. The child kept repeating the phrase until Kim rocked her like a baby and she was still.

Desperately Kim looked at Daphne and saw the pity there. Then she looked at Candy's father, but she could read nothing into the blankness that was his face.

At last she put Candy down. "Come up to bed, Candy, and I'll show you what I've brought you. It's a big, thick note-book and a packet of pencils, and you can write lots and lots of stories . . ."

When Candy was in bed, quiet, contentedly asleep, Kim went downstairs at Owen's request. She had still had no food. She felt now that she could not face it.

"Sit down, Miss Paton." She did, thankfully. "I know it sounds ironic and perhaps a little belated to say this after the scene we have just witnessed, but don't let my daughter get too tied to your apron-strings."

Kim paused before she answered, having to gather her scattered wits. "Is that a piece of advice, Mr. Lang — or a warning?"

There was a short silence, then, "A warning, Miss Paton, a dire warning."

"Meaning, Mr. Lang?"

"Meaning that I won't have my daughter become emotionally entangled with anyone I employ."

"Have you," she asked sarcastically, "some magic formula to prevent its happening? Do you intend to dose me with some nasty medicine to make me repulsive to her and stop her getting too fond of me?"

He sighed, "I only wish I could, Miss Paton."

Her response was to rest her elbows on her knees and drop her head into her hands. She thought she had taken as much as she could, but apparently there was more to come — a fencing match with the father.

"And I'll tell you why," he went on softly to her bent head. "I'm afraid. In fact, I'm terrified. You're young, you're –" there was a tiny pause, "attractive. You're just passing through. You're not a permanent fixture in my household. Some time you'll find a man you want to marry, so you'll leave. Then what?"

She raised her head and said quietly, "Doesn't it occur to you that I might also have your daughter's interest at heart? That I might have grown fond of *her*?"

She knew immediately that she had said the wrong thing. His smile was distorted by cynicism. He asked softly, "What are you after, Miss Paton?"

She got up wearily. She should have known that, in Owen Lang's language, what she had just said was tantamount to making love to him and asking him to marry her.

She wondered as she climbed the stairs and flung herself on to the bed, if she could stand it much longer.

A few days after her return, Owen told her, "I'm bringing a colleague home to dinner this evening." He did not apologise for the short notice. "This time there will be no need for my daughter to have her meal with you. We won't be talking business."

"Yes, Mr. Lang," she answered. Or perhaps it should have been "No, Mr. Lang." Relations between them were so strained these days, she was never sure how to address him. Everything she said seemed to displease him.

When she told Candy what her father had said, Candy rebelled. "I don't want to sit in there and listen to a silly old man talking to my daddy."

But when the colleague arrived, it was not a "silly old man" who walked in the door. It was a slim, graceful woman in her early thirties. Her hair was blonde and drawn back in a French pleat. Her face was high-boned and striking, but her mouth and eyes had about them a calculating hardness which came near to destroying the beauty of feature which was undoubtedly hers.

The rest of her was in accord with her superficial attractiveness and her dress, which she must have put on before leaving work, was in a gaily patterned summer-cool style well suited to the warmer weather they were having. She made Kim, in her serviceable navy and white which she had thought fit to wear in the circumstances, feel almost dowdy.

Briefly Owen introduced them. "Berenice, this is my housekeeper, Kim Paton. Miss Paton, my friend and colleague, Berenice Randall."

Kim noticed his description of the woman with a sinking heart. So she was his "friend", was she? Soon, obviously, she would be more than friend. As she felt the woman's limp hand rest momentarily in hers, Kim remembered her employer's promise on her birthday at the lakeside. "I shall take your advice – I'll find my daughter a mother."

He had kept his promise. This woman was his choice and she was one of those rare creatures he had so desired and almost despaired of finding – both intelligent and beautiful and therefore, in his opinion, fitted in every way to become his wife. She was, in his own words, "a dream come true."

Candy appeared from behind Kim. "And this," said the woman called Berenice, in silvery tones, "I'm sure, is Candy. What a sweet little girl!" She held out her hand. "Candy, I'm so pleased to see you at last. I've heard so much about you."

But Candy refused to co-operate. Her hand stayed obstinately behind her back. The guest laughed charmingly and gave her an understanding pat. Owen, his hand on her arm, led Berenice into the sitting-room.

"Miss Paton," he said over his shoulder, "we shall have a drink, then I assume the meal will be ready?"

"Yes, of course, Mr. Lang." She spoke in her most servant-like manner. Fleetingly, their eyes met, hers docile, his suspicious, then he joined his guest.

Judging the time to perfection, Kim carried in the food and served it with the expertise she had acquired during the weeks she had been working for Owen Lang. True to her lowly status, she endeavoured to fade into the background as her employer and his visitor chatted and small-talked and Candy fidgeted in her chair.

Candy tried to catch her eye, but Kim obstinately kept hers down. She slid out of the room, sidling round the door like a purring cat rubbing itself against the wood, and served the next course in the same style.

She thought she caught a questioning look now and then on the face of her employer, but she herself maintained a serious and dedicated expression, as if that moment was all she had lived for.

It was during the second half of the meal that she heard Candy's shrill, argumentative voice. "I want to finish my dinner with Kim."

"Be quiet!" her father snapped, his angry tone penetrating the closed door.

"*I want to finish my dinner with Kim!*" This time it was a shriek.

"You're staying right here, my girl!" Kim had never heard Owen talk to his daughter so sternly and it had the effect she expected.

There was a howl and a shout — he might even have struck her. "I *hate* you! I hate *her*!" She no doubt meant her future stepmother. "And I want Kim. I'm going to Kim!"

The dining-room door was torn open and Kim stood in readiness for whatever happened next. Candy almost fell into the kitchen. She threw herself on Kim, clutched her round the waist and buried her face against her.

Owen strode in, Berenice following. "Let my daughter go, Miss Paton!"

Kim said coolly, "I have no control over the situation, Mr. Lang. As you could see if you were to look closely." She raised her arms to demonstrate.

"Don't let her talk to you like that, Owen," came a scandalised voice from behind him. "She's only a servant."

"Candy," said her father, his voice like sandpaper, "let go of Miss Paton and *come back with me*!"

"She's not Miss Paton," came the defiant, muffled answer, "she's Kim. And I'm staying with her."

It was fortunate for Candy that she could not see the look of violence which took possession of her father's eyes, but Kim did, and put her arms protectively round the little figure.

"Let my daughter go, Miss Paton," Owen said through his teeth, "or I'll –" He raised his hand.

"If you touch a hair of the child's head, Mr. Lang," Kim's voice came steadily, quietly, belying the terror which was curdling her blood, "I shall take her next door to Daphne's and keep her there."

He paled. "You're defying *me*, Miss Paton? *You dare to defy me?*" His anger burst through like the breaching of a dam. He lifted his hand again, this time swung it, giving her a stinging slap on the cheek. Her lip quivered, her eyes filled, but she stood her ground. She would rather have taken the blow than have had it borne by the child she was protecting.

As the moment passed, he realised what he had done. He looked at his hand, he looked at her cheek, saw the painful redness spreading over the skin. His anger receded, leaving him dazed and drained of life. He turned and walked slowly from the kitchen.

Candy moved away at last, into the hall and up the stairs, her footsteps thumping each tread. But Kim remained standing, pale and shaking. She thought, "This is the end. It must be. He won't keep me now."

And misery swamped her. She could not love him less because of what he had done. She felt perhaps she loved him even more. Now she knew that under the cynicism and coldness of his manner, he possessed a passion as impetuous and uncontrollable as any other man's.

Somehow she composed herself enough to take in the coffee. While she poured it out, there was a deathly silence. Berenice gave her a cold, haughty stare, but Owen did not look up.

Candy went to bed early, probably, Kim guessed, to keep out of her father's way. It was not late when Owen took Berenice home. Kim sat in the kitchen, a book open but unread on the table in front of her, awaiting his return.

CHAPTER VIII

HE came in quietly and went into the dining-room. Then there was silence. It took all the courage Kim possessed to seek him out. She found the dining-room door half open. Owen was seated at the table, elbows on it, his head in his hands.

For a few moments she stood in the doorway watching him with a deep compassion. She had decided to withdraw quietly when he must have heard her.

"What do you want?" His voice was belligerent, his face haggard.

She had no choice now but to go in. She took a breath, braced herself and said, "I want to say I'm sorry, Mr. Lang. I want to apologise for defying you. I had no right to do what I did, or say what I did, especially in the circumstances, in front of your guest."

The way he lifted his head to look at her it must have seemed to him to weigh a ton. "When you've quite finished abasing yourself, perhaps you'll give me a chance to speak. I too am sorry for what happened, for what I did. Now we're quits."

There was a painful silence. "Do you — want me to leave, Mr. Lang? If so, I'll go and pack right away."

Somehow she had raised his ire again. "Do I want you to leave? My God, I've never wanted anyone to leave so much before! But I'm stuck with you, aren't I? Whether I want you or not, you've got to stay. Because of my daughter, that's why. You know damned well that if you went, she'd go with you. Or run away and try to find you."

Kim shook her head helplessly, holding out her hands in a gesture of appeal. "But what can I do?"

"Do? Nothing, absolutely nothing. I told you the other day I was terrified. Now perhaps you see what I mean."

She started to speak but he snapped, "Oh, go away. Get out

135

and leave me alone!"

She left him alone.

Candy had her birthday party. Three days before, invitations were handed round at school to seven little friends, and three days later, seven small girls were deposited by their mothers on the doorstep and a riotous party followed.

Beyond giving his daughter a present – a new blue frilly party dress and large walking-talking doll – Owen took no interest in the proceedings. On Candy's birthday morning, he appeared at breakfast apparently happy and cheerful, but on looking at him closely, Kim realised what an effort it was costing him. He looked on sourly as Candy, in a state of mesmerised rapture, unwrapped Kim's present – an "Eskimo" doll in a fur-trimmed scarlet coat and hood and long grey fur-trimmed skirt with two tiny dolls strapped securely to her back.

"It's a mummy doll with her babies, Daddy." She thrust the gift under his nose and he jerked back as if he could not bear to look at it. He fixed a smile on his face, praising it in tones that satisfied Candy, then gave his housekeeper a sarcastic stare – she could guess what was in his mind, that it was yet another subtle hint on her part that Candy needed a mother – and shut her out again with his morning paper.

When Candy came out of school that day, she could hardly contain her excitement. She raced upstairs to change into her new dress and rushed down to greet her guests with a smile and a welcoming word, hostess to her finger-tips.

Kim supervised everything – the games, the competitions, the tea. She had spent the day making cakes and trifles and sandwiches, cooking sausages and spiking them on sticks.

The ceremony of the candle-blowing was conducted with great solemnity and everyone clapped when all seven were extinguished at once after a deep breath and a noisy blow.

Towards the end of the party, Owen came home. He stood in the doorway and watched Kim organising and directing the games, encouraging the losers and praising the winners. When the mothers came to collect their offspring he retreated unnoticed into a corner.

With desperate, envious eyes, Candy watched as her little guests hung round their mothers, chatting to them, showing them the sweets and gifts they had won. At last, as if she could not hold herself back any longer, Candy rushed across to Kim and hung on to her arm.

"My mummy," she announced, "this is my mummy." She looked up with appealing, triumphant eyes into Kim's face and tugged her down to kiss her. Owen pushed his way out of the room.

The other children laughed at Candy, the mothers looked fleetingly compassionate, then forgot the incident immediately as they ushered out their loved ones.

The party was over. Candy was in bed and Kim was alone. The washing-up had to be faced. Kim loaded the dishwasher, but even when it was full, there were some items left over. She switched on. Nothing happened. She switched off and tried again. No response. Oh no, Kim thought, it could not have gone wrong *now*!

But it had. Tired beyond belief, hardly able to stand because of aching legs and throbbing head, she painstakingly unloaded the dishwasher and filled the sink with water. One by one she washed the pieces of crockery. More than half an hour later, she was still washing up.

She heard a noise from the doorway. Owen was watching her, astonished. "Why do it by hand?"

She motioned to the dishwasher. "It's gone wrong."

"It hasn't! Not now!" He walked across and inspected it. Like Kim, he could get nothing out of it. "Damn!" he said. "It would choose now."

He took the tea towel from the rail and started drying up.

"It doesn't matter, Mr. Lang," Kim said wearily. "I'll get it all done in time."

He ignored her statement and carried on. There was silence for some time, broken only by the clatter of crockery and cutlery.

Then Owen said, "I should be glad if you would disenchant my daughter, Miss Paton."

Too tired to fence, but having to take him up on his statement, she asked, "About what?"

"About the fact that you're not her mother."

Aroused now, she turned on him. "Can't you see that the claim she made in front of all those children was born of desperation – that they had mothers and she couldn't bear to be the odd one out? You can hardly fail to have noticed by now how she clings to me. She can't seem to bear me out of her sight."

He asked softly, baitingly, "Are you trying to tell me in a roundabout way that you've become so indispensable to her that you're now a permanent fixture in this house? That you now have me where you want me, and that I have no alternative but to marry you?" He went on with cynicism, "I must congratulate you on an entirely new approach. None of the others thought of that."

She turned towards him, her wet hands resting on the edge of the sink. "Mr. Lang, I state categorically here and now, and I hope for the last time, that I have no intention of marrying you, I have no wish to marry you, and that the very thought of sharing your life with you until death us do part positively sickens me. Does that satisfy you?"

She turned back to her work. She could not go on talking because of the lump in her throat. Now she might just as well crawl away and die. She had told him some lies in the past, but the lie she had just uttered was the biggest of them all. Her "veils", he called them. Well, this was a veil that would never be torn down as long as she lived.

He stayed until the drying up was finished. Slumped in a chair, head down, she thanked him for his help.

"Miss Paton?" She looked up. "You're deathly tired. Come into my sitting-room and rest."

"No, thank you. I don't feel like small talk."

"I don't either. But I'll give you a drink. Come along."
She did not move. He said quietly, "It's an order, Miss Paton."

She knew from his tone she had to obey. She swayed with tiredness as she walked along the hall and his arm went round her waist to steady her. He sat her in an armchair and put a drink into her hand. She took it without a word.

The silence was peaceful and soothing. He broke it by thanking her for giving his daughter the first party she had ever had.

She passed it off lightly. "I did it for Candy."

"I'm well aware," he replied, "that you didn't do it for me." He rested his head on the back of the chair and looked at her, his eyes half-closed. "I wanted a housekeeper who couldn't stand the sight of me, didn't I? And by heaven, I've got one!"

She had nothing to say on the subject. She found her eyes closing and he rose and took away her empty glass. "Another drink, Kim?"

She shook her head, too tired to respond even to his use of her first name. Her head drooped and she felt him lift it and put a cushion into place to support it. In the silence and the stillness, she slept . . .

She felt herself being lifted and carried, mounting the stairs, the roughness of a man's jacket beneath her cheek, soft breath against her face. She was being lowered on to a bed, her shoes removed and a quilt pulled over her.

She heard a whispered, "Goodnight, Kim, and thanks again," heard herself reply, "Goodnight Owen." And she turned on her side and dreamed of him the whole night through.

She awoke next morning to find her dress crumpled and all her clothes still on. It took a few seconds to work out why. Then she grew hot with embarrassment and she realised what must have happened. Owen must have grown exasperated at having to wait for her to wake up before he himself could go to bed, so he had carried her upstairs and dumped her down and left her.

She apologised when she saw him at breakfast. He merely shrugged behind his newspaper. That afternoon Candy handed her a note from school, informing her that a school concert was being held in a few days' time and the headmistress would welcome all parents at two o'clock.

"I'm in it," Candy explained. "I'm playing the recorder. Will you come, Kim? *Please*, Kim. No one's ever been before, because Daddy's always at work in the daytime." She added sadly, "Other children's mummies always come."

Kim had a swift mental picture of a lonely little girl, enviously eyeing the doors of the school hall, watching all the other mothers arrive but never her own. It made Kim want to cry.

"Of course I'll come, Candy. That is, if your daddy doesn't mind."

"He won't, he won't mind, Kim."

But Kim was not so sure. That evening, she tackled him. She explained about the school concert and asked, could she go?

"There's no need. You would be exceeding your duties if you do. I employ you as housekeeper, not part-time mother."

"But if I don't go, Candy will be terribly upset. In fact, she already believes I'm going."

"Look," he was growing irritated, "if you've made up your mind to go – and it's obvious you have – why did you bother to ask me?"

"Are you saying in a roundabout way that I can go?"

"Oh, make your own decision, for heaven's sake. You usually do in the end. You, Miss Paton, are a law unto yourself. I've never come across anyone like you."

"Thank you so much, Mr. Lang," she said primly. He raised an eyebrow, obviously unsure whether she was thanking him for his permission to attend the concert, or his sarcastic comment.

He called her back as she reached the kitchen. "Tomorrow evening I'm having Daphne and Hamish South in. I'm also inviting my colleague, Berenice Randall."

"I see." Her throat tightened. Did that mean she was being left out of the social gathering? "You want me to prepare food, savouries and so on, and coffee?"

"Of course. That's what I pay you for, isn't it?" He added, baiting her, "Provided it's not too much trouble."

She slammed the door on his sarcasm.

Berenice arrived first. Owen was upstairs when she came, so Kim had to open the door to her. Berenice gave her a cold stare, which was clearly intended to let Kim know she had not forgotten her display of mutiny the last time she was there. Kim took the coat which was removed with a flourish to reveal a clinging white sleeveless dress. No one could deny her beauty, Kim thought, which, backed by the brains it seemed she possessed, made her formidable opposition for any woman, let alone a lowly domestic servant, as Kim had ruefully come to regard herself.

Owen greeted Berenice as he came down the stairs, handsome, neat yet casually dressed, smiling, his hand outstretched as though the engagement ring was already on her finger.

Kim could not bear to witness the meeting, so she went quickly into the kitchen. When the doorbell rang again, she hurried to open it with a smile.

"My dear Kim," said Daphne, "lovely to see you again. It's – how long – all of two days, isn't it?"

Hamish laughed. "A lifetime," he commented. They found hooks for their coats without troubling Kim. When she showed them into the sitting-room to join the others, they hesitated at the door. They had not expected to see a stranger there. When Kim started to withdraw, Daphne turned back and whispered, "Kim?"

But Kim shook her head. Hamish frowned, obviously displeased and puzzled. It was as much as he could do, judging by his expression, to stop himself saying "What's this? No Kim?" But at his wife's cautionary look he subsided.

There was chatter and laughter and the chink of glasses. Kim heard it all as she sat in the kitchen arranging the food on plates and the coffee cups on a tray. Then, having nothing better to do, she stared out at the garden. Dusk was closing up the flowers and stilling all movement. The sky was cloudless and blue grey as darkness hovered, awaiting the right moment to oust the last remnants of daylight.

She turned from the window and found herself near to tears. If this was a form of punishment thought up by Owen for her misdeeds as his rebellious housekeeper, then he was hitting where it really hurt. He had shut her out with the deliberation of a prison warder closing a cell door. He had put her socially beneath not only himself, but his friends and neighbours.

Daphne crept in and closed the kitchen door. "My dear," she said, "why?"

Kim shook her head, too miserable to speak.

"What goes on between you? Didn't he invite you in?"

"No. He invited his 'friend and colleague', as he calls her. He should have said his future wife and stepmother for Candy."

Hamish appeared. "What the hell are you talking about? Who's that glamorous, completely nauseating female he's got in there? Why aren't you in there with us?"

To all three questions, Kim could only shrug in answer.

"He left her out, Hamish," his wife explained. "What do you mean, Kim? Is he going to marry her?"

"I couldn't tell you. I suppose I brought it on myself, partly. On my birthday we went for a picnic – at Candy's suggestion – and I told him he ought to provide a mother for her. He said he would take my advice. Hence the glamorous female."

"But he can't marry *her*," Hamish yelped. "A hard-bitten, calculating, supercilious –" He stopped. "I won't say it, because she's a guest like us, but honestly, Kim, all she seems to be able to talk about is how clever she is at her job, what a wonderful boss Owen is and what a darling little daughter he has."

"From which one can gather," said Kim with unaccustomed cynicism, "that she's got the message. She already regards herself as his wife-to-be and is rehearsing for the part."

Hamish tightened his lips. "You wait till I get Owen alone. I'll tell him exactly what I think of him."

"Darling," said his wife, "what he does with his life is not our business."

"Isn't it? Then I'll damned well make it my business. There's our Kim here, left out in the cold . . ."

"Miss Paton." Owen was standing at the kitchen door looking at them. "When you're ready and when you can spare the time from entertaining your friends . . ."

"Look here, Owen!" Hamish turned on him, but Daphne

caught his arm.

"Darling," she said, smiling sweetly at her husband, "we mustn't neglect Owen's dear friend and colleague. We're so sorry, Owen, we were just taking time off to have a chat with a friend of ours . . ."

"Miss Paton!" Owen turned his fury on to her. "I take it you *have* provided some food and drink for us and that you will be kind enough to condescend to bring it in now?"

Hamish opened his mouth to protest at Owen's tone, but his wife tugged him from the room, whispering soothing words in his ear.

"Yes, Mr. Lang," Kim said wearily. "That's what you pay me for, isn't it, Mr. Lang?"

Hamish overheard and gave one guffaw of laughter. The rest must have been speedily smothered by his wife.

Owen gave her a shrivelling look and strode back to his guests. Kim trundled the trolley laden with food and drink along the hall and tapped on the sitting-room door. Hamish opened it.

"Coming to join us, Kim?" he asked loudly, but at his wife's sharp "Hamish!" he subsided into his chair.

"Leave it, Miss Paton," said Owen. "Miss Randall will act as hostess."

"With pleasure, Mr. Lang," Kim replied, putting undue emphasis on the "pleasure" part. The choke of laughter which came from Hamish's throat acted as a balm to soothe away the pain which Owen's words had inflicted.

The rest of the evening crawled by. The guests stayed late, and before Daphne went home she put her head round the kitchen door and said loudly, "You must come in one evening for a chat, Kim – alone."

Owen took Berenice home and returned while Kim was supervising the dishwasher which by now had been repaired. He went straight up to bed, leaving her to it. It was then, and only then, that she allowed herself to droop and acknowledge defeat.

When Kim dropped Candy at school on the day of the concert, Candy said, over and over again, "Don't forget, two o'clock."

Kim promised to be on time and, after an early lunch, she drove to the school and found a seat in the front row. As Candy's class entered and took their places round the sides of the hall, Kim watched Candy, looking like a lost lamb hunting desperately for its mother, search the gathering of parents and grandparents for a sight of her face.

As she spotted Kim at last, her anxiety gave way to a glow of delight. Kim was deeply touched and searched for her handkerchief, blowing her nose and hoping that no one had noticed her dabbing at her eyes.

When it was Candy's turn to play with the recorder group, she filed on to the platform and kept her eyes fastened on to Kim until she had to withdraw them to follow the music.

It was a lighthearted piece they performed at first, followed by a melancholy air. The sweet, sad notes the children produced echoed movingly around the hall, forcing Kim's thoughts inwards to an open acknowledgement of the torment that was eating deep into her subconscious mind and, if she allowed it, threatening to destroy her entire happiness, both present and future.

She felt trapped, both emotionally and physically, like a wild bird in captivity. She had to get out, to break free. She could not stand it much longer, torn in two as she was by her love for a child and her father on the one hand, and on the other, the kind of life she really wanted to lead.

That job her brother had mentioned – she would write and tell him she was prepared to accept it. As soon as Candy was in bed, she would write that letter. She did not allow herself to consider the consequences of such an action.

The concert was over. Candy was smiling and smiling. As she filed out with the others, she gave a secret wave, which Kim returned. One of the teachers noticed the exchange and as Kim passed her in the corridor, she put her hand on Kim's arm and drew her into a room marked "Headmistress".

The woman apologised for her action, explained that she was Miss Calder, the head teacher, and had come to the conclusion that Kim was connected in some way with Candida Lang. "Are you," Miss Calder asked hopefully, "her step-mother?"

"No, I'm not."

Miss Calder looked disappointed. "Are you, by any chance, the person she calls 'Kim'?" Kim nodded. "We've asked her 'who's Kim, a friend?' and she told us, 'No, she's the lady who looks after me.'"

Kim explained that she was the housekeeper.

"Well," Miss Calder laughed, "you must have made a deep impression on her, because she writes about you in her stories and in her 'news'. It's nothing but 'Kim, Kim'!" She regarded Kim closely. "I hope you don't object to my asking, but are you staying? It seems she's had so many changes, the poor child has no sense of security at all. She's very emotional at school, and easily upset, which is a pity because she's a very intelligent little girl. With a more secure background we're sure she could do really well."

"I – don't know whether I shall be staying," Kim answered cautiously, pulling at her collar as though it was a rope round her neck.

"Oh, I do hope so, for Candy's sake. She's so good at writing, you know. Words flow from her, she can't seem to keep them back – quite remarkable for her age."

Kim said, "You do know her father is a scientist and insists that she will follow in his footsteps?"

Miss Calder said ruefully, "My dear, I know. Every time he comes to an open evening and sees her work, he tells us. But all her inclination is the other way. It's a problem, it really is. Of course," she looked at Kim optimistically, "that's where a mother would come in useful – to argue with Candy's father!"

Kim promised she would do her best to encourage Candy with her story writing and the headmistress laughingly said she hoped they would see much more of Candy's 'Kim' at the school.

Kim waited outside for Candy, and watched her come skipping out of the door with a crowd of friends. She ran up to Kim joyfully. "Did I play all right? Did you like the music?"

On the way home, Kim told her how much she had enjoyed it. Later, Owen listened to Kim's account of what the head teacher had said with growing cynicism.

"Writes stories? Good at English? What the hell's the use of that in this scientific age?"

Kim said, trying to pass it off as a joke but refusing to look at him, "Miss Calder said Candy needed a mother to argue with Candy's father!"

"Offering your services?" came softly, maddeningly from her employer.

There he goes again, she thought with a sigh, but I suppose I asked for it. She said, with a half-smile, "It would be all the same if I were, wouldn't it?"

"You never said a truer word, Miss Paton!" Now he was smiling. "Well," he stood, towering over her as she sat despondently in one of his armchairs, "there's only one way out of the situation. Since I've vowed never to marry any housekeeper of mine, and you in any case have an unrelenting aversion to all scientists, especially me, with all possible speed I shall have to propose marriage to my friend and colleague, Berenice Randall." He waited for Kim's reaction. None came. "Won't I, Miss Paton?"

"That, Mr. Lang," she stood and raised her eyes with difficulty to meet his, "would seem to be the only solution." She went quickly from the room.

As soon as Candy was in bed, she promised herself, she would write that letter accepting the job. Candy snuggled down into the bedclothes and flung up her arms, pulling Kim down towards her. She whispered into Kim's ear,

"When the other girls asked me who you were, do you know what I told them?" Afraid of the answer, Kim shook her head. "I said you were my mummy – my new mummy."

Kim's hand flew to her neck. Now the rope around it had tightened into a stranglehold. She kissed Candy goodnight and went to her room. She wrote that letter – regretfully turning the job down.

Next morning Owen emerged from behind his newspaper to

open a letter the postman had delivered. "It would seem," he announced, "that my parents are wishing themselves on us for one night. They appear to be passing near the area on their way to the south coast for a short holiday."

Candy clapped her hands. "Are my granny and grandpa coming?"

"They are." He turned to Kim, "So, Miss Paton, despite the short notice – they're arriving tomorrow, good thing it's Saturday when I'll be home – you will have to prepare a room for them. They usually have the one next to mine."

All the way to school, Candy chatted about her grand-parents. "They always bring me presents and sweets. They haven't been for ages."

Kim dusted and cleaned the spare bedroom and even washed the curtains. She made up the bed and put flowers in the room. She parked her car in the road again so that they could put theirs in the drive. When they arrived, Kim heard them ask who owned the little red car at the kerb.

"My housekeeper," she heard her employer say.

His parents made noises of surprise. He called her out of the kitchen to meet them. They shook her hand warmly and looked at her with keen, shrewd eyes.

Owen's mother was small, comfortably proportioned and had a look of the confirmed optimist. His father was tall and white-haired and quietly-spoken. For goodness' sake, Kim thought, who does he take after – not these two charming people!

"Miss Paton?" said Mrs. Lang.

"It's Kim, it's Kim!" cried Candy, jumping up and down and hugging her grandparents in turn.

"Kim, is it? Then we'll call her Kim, like Candy does. Much more friendly!"

Kim looked at Owen. "Shall I show your parents to their room, Mr. Lang?"

"My dear," commented his mother, "we know our way blindfold. But do come up and we can have a little chat."

"Miss Paton had better stay downstairs," said her son coldly. "She has the lunch to prepare."

Mrs. Lang looked at her son a little oddly. "The meal can wait a few minutes, Owen. I'd like to get to know this young lady who has surely stayed here as your housekeeper for an extraordinary length of time. I want to know how she's managed to put up with you for so long!" Her son turned away sharply and went into the kitchen himself.

Kim picked up the cases to carry them upstairs, but Mrs. Lang told her, "Put them down immediately, Kim. I'll get my son to bring those up. Can't have a slim young girl like you carrying such heavy cases."

Owen emerged from the kitchen and carried the cases upstairs with bad grace. Somehow his mother seemed to have upset him. Candy claimed her grandfather and pulled him into the garden.

Mrs. Lang sat on the bed and glanced round appreciatively.

"You really have made the room look inviting, my dear. Thank you for the lovely flowers." She looked Kim up and down in a kindly manner. "And how are you getting on with my difficult son?"

"Not – too badly," was the hesitant answer, and his mother laughed.

"How very loyal of you to say that! I'm quite sure he makes life very difficult for you. Even as a boy he was very hard to please. Always seeking perfection, although I told him that was something he would never find as long as he lived!"

Kim laughed with something like relief. This woman knew her son only too well. "He is awkward at times, Mrs. Lang. We – we have our clashes. We don't always see eye to eye."

"You quarrel with him? Now that means you have spirit, which is something I always admire. Tell me, what do you quarrel about?"

"Well, to be honest, almost everything!"

Mrs. Lang laughed heartily, enjoying the joke. "And yet you're still here? My word, it seems he's been needing someone like you to bring him down to earth."

Kim looked at her watch. "I'll get back to the kitchen, if you will excuse me."

"Certainly. I'll unpack, then I'll be down to give you a hand."

"Oh, there's no need for that, Mrs. Lang. I don't think your son would like it, anyway."

"My son," said his mother with a smile, "will have to like it, or do the other thing, my dear Kim!"

Kim laughed and ran down the stairs feeling happier than she had felt for a long time. She was glad to find the kitchen empty. She thought that perhaps Owen was there trying to supervise the meal.

Soon, Mrs. Lang bustled in, an apron covering her skirt. "Now, what about the table? Is it set? No? I'll do it, then. Let me see, there are five of us, aren't there?"

"Five? No, four, Mrs. Lang. I have my meals in here."

"You *what*? My dear child, you're eating with us. I'll not have you sitting alone out here."

"But your son insists —"

"Then my son will have to stop insisting. What century is he living in, for goodness' sake?" Owen appeared, looking annoyed. "Do you think we're still in the Victorian era, Owen?" his mother asked indignantly. "Making your housekeeper have her meals out here, as though you were some great overlord and she a lowly maidservant!"

"But, Mother, it's my business where my housekeeper eats."

"Not when I'm staying with you it isn't. Kim is eating with us in the dining-room. You need humanising, my boy. It's time some woman took you in hand!"

His mother pushed past him as he stood in the doorway and as she disappeared into the dining-room, he gave Kim a crushing look, which was so unjustified it goaded Kim into snapping,

"If you think it was my idea, Mr. Lang, then you're wrong. I'm sure I won't enjoy a mouthful having to share a table with you!"

He growled, "Miss Paton, I —"

"That's right, Kim," came a voice from the dining-room, "put my son in his place!"

149

Owen made a threatening movement with his fist towards his housekeeper and turned and stormed upstairs to his bedroom.

Mrs. Lang returned, saying blandly, "Let him sulk a little while, Kim. It will do him good."

Kim laughed at her tactics, yet quailed inside at what might happen to her when Owen's parents had gone away again.

Candy pulled her grandfather in from the garden. "Here's Kim!" she shouted, ebullient in her happiness.

Owen's father tutted goodhumouredly. "It's been Kim, Kim, the whole time. You really must be a wonderful young lady."

"She is," cried Candy. "She gave me a birthday party and made me a cake with seven candles."

"She did?" Mrs. Lang, returning from the dining-room, was sincerely surprised.

"And she takes me to school in her car and collects me. And she came to hear me play the recorder at the school concert. And I told all my friends –" She stopped, uncertain now, her large blue eyes looking appealingly from one grandparent to the other, knowing in her heart that what she was about to say was nothing but an impossible dream. She finished in a whisper, "I told them she was my mummy – my new mumy."

"Oh, my dear!" Mrs. Lang's eyes filled and she turned away quickly.

Lawrence Lang did not even try to hide his dismay. "But –" he began, but his wife flapped her hand and murmured "Hush!"

Owen chose that moment to appear. "Where's my lunch? I'm hungry." He stared at the silent group. "Why so quiet?"

His mother came to life. "Take Candy into the dining-room, Owen. Lunch is ready."

"I can take myself," Candy said indignantly, "I'm a big girl now."

"Lawrence," Mrs. Lang said to her husband, "keep her amused while we dish up."

When they had gone, Mrs. Lang turned to Kim. "My dear

young lady, you have a problem. You certainly have a problem."

During lunch, Kim sat opposite Owen, but she kept her eyes away from him, knowing she would only find censure there.

'The plants and apple trees look healthy," commented Lawrence Lang. He looked at Kim. "Who's the gardener in this house? Not my son, I'll bet."

"It's Uncle Hamish," Candy announced.

"Candy!" Kim reprimanded her gently.

"But he is," she said in an injured tone. "Every time Kim goes out there, he comes in and does it for her."

They all laughed, including Owen, to Kim's surprise.

"I think," said Mrs. Lang, "Candy's telling tales. I'm sure Kim does most of it."

"Well —" Kim said, and rose to collect the dishes, hoping to end the conversation. Mrs. Lang got up too. "Don't bother, Mrs. Lang. I'll do it. It's my job."

"Nonsense." Mrs. Lang seized some plates. "When I come to see my family, I don't just come to sit around and look pretty."

Kim stole a look at Owen to see how he was taking the subtle insinuation that she was part of the family. His expression was neutral.

After lunch, Candy's grandfather took her to the local park and Owen went with them. Mrs. Lang invited Kim to join her in the sitting-room. "Now, Kim, we're alone at last. Tell me about yourself. Where is your home, and how did you come to get this job?"

Feeling trapped, she answered cautiously, "There isn't much to tell."

But Owen's mother used the same tone with her as she used with her son. She put on a "no nonsense" voice and said, "I don't believe that, young lady. I can see you're different. I've noticed something unusual about you ever since I came. You're not the real 'housekeeper' type. I've seen too many of my son's to know that." She looked at Kim shrewdly. "You shouldn't really be here at all, should you?"

Slowly Kim answered, "Mrs. Lang, if I tell you, you must promise not to breathe a word of it to Owen." If Mrs. Lang noticed her use of his first name, she did not let it show.

"I promise, my dear. You can trust me implicitly."

So, with a deep sense of relief, Kim told Owen's mother everything – about her family, her degree, her struggle between her affection for Candy (she said nothing about her love for Candy's father) and wanting to break away and take a job more suited to her qualifications.

"My dear," Mrs. Lang said when Kim had finished, "this is a greater problem than I realised. Have you discussed it with your parents?"

"With my mother, yes. She said she didn't know what to advise."

"I sympathise with her. But there is one solution." Mrs. Lang looked closely at Kim and shook her head. "It wouldn't be fair, though, to tie you down all your life, your career in front of you. It couldn't be expected of you."

Kim knew what she had in mind and was glad that she had not spoken her thoughts aloud. The solution Mrs. Lang had in mind was, to Kim, as much an unattainable dream as Candy's longing that she, Kim, would ever become her mother.

"Unfortunately," Mrs. Lang went on, "my son was soured by his first experience of marriage. He married the wrong woman – she let him down badly and even after Candy was born, things seemed no better. She wouldn't settle down and be a proper wife to him."

When the others returned, Mrs. Lang said to her son with great satisfaction, "Your charming housekeeper and I have had a lovely chat. Now we understand each other much better."

Owen looked suspicious and followed Kim into the kitchen. "What's all this about a woman-to-woman chat? What has my mother been doing in her usual interfering way – marrying you off to me?"

"Your mother, Mr. Lang," she said in tones as icy as his, "is far too sensible a woman to want to wish a boorish, churlish, ill-mannered man on me for life, even though that man may be her son."

152

He snarled, "By heaven, if my parents weren't here I'd make you pay for that bit of insolence. In talking to me like that you're simply taking advantage of their presence here. Don't provoke me too far, Miss Paton, or you'll regret it. I'm still master in my own house, even though my mother appears temporarily to have taken possession of it – and its occupants."

"I'm sorry, Mr. Lang," she turned her back on him and started getting the tea ready, "if you regard what I've said as insolence. It was in fact the truth. The way you've just spoken to me is proof of it."

She heard the hiss of indrawn breath and the kitchen door slammed. As soon as he had gone, she began to feel sorry for the way she had abused him, and felt the urge to run after him and apologise, but the circumstances prevented it.

Later, when Candy was in bed and Owen's father was in the garden talking to Hamish and Daphne over the garden fence, Mrs. Lang tackled her son.

"Owen, my dear, something's got to be done. You can't just let things drift." He appeared to be puzzled and asked what she was talking about. "The situation that prevails in your household at present. You've got to consider Kim – she won't be with you for ever, you know."

"Well?" His face was wooden. "What do you want me to do – lock her in every time I go to work, in case she ups and leaves while I'm away?"

"Don't be cynical, son. This is serious. Candy's formed such a strong attachment to her that, frankly, I don't know the answer."

"It's simple." He was being cynical again. "I'll just have to keep employing her to satisfy my daughter's emotional requirements. Then when Candy is old enough to do without a substitute mother, I can dispense with her services and throw her out."

His mother looked shocked at his careless attitude. "What about this Berenice person I've heard you're friendly with?"

He stiffened. "Who told you about her? My housekeeper?" He gave Kim a murderous look. "I thought so. She should learn to mind her own business and stop interfering in my

153

private life."

"Don't be silly, son, Kim is part of your private life. She's part of your home." Owen seemed speechless. He flung his book on the floor and walked up and down the room.

"Well, Owen," his mother went on mildly, noting his restlessness with interest, "this Berenice – is she a possibility?"

"I suppose you're now talking about my remarriage? And discussing it as though it were a business arrangement with no feelings, no emotional involvement."

"All I want to know, son," his mother persisted quietly, "is, do you like her – love her, in fact, enough to marry her and thus let Kim go?"

He swung round and turned on Kim. "Will you get out, Miss Paton? However much my mother tries to pretend you're one of the family, I know damned well you're not. I pay you to work, not to listen in on a family discussion."

Kim rose and made for the door.

"Owen," his mother chided, "you mustn't speak to her like that, you really mustn't. You don't realise . . ."

"Mrs. Lang! Please . . ."

Owen's mother knew at once why Kim was appealing to her. She shook her head. "It's all right, my dear, don't worry."

And Kim knew she understood. She had promised not to breathe a word to Owen about Kim's secrets and Kim knew she could be trusted.

As she closed the door, Kim heard Mrs. Lang say, "You really must be more polite to her, son."

"More polite!" came an exasperated shout. "Good grief, you should hear the way she talks to me sometimes!"

Sick at heart, Kim wandered into the garden.

"What's up?" Daphne asked. "His Nibs been at it again? And with his parents here, too?"

Mrs. Lang soon joined them. It seemed she had got nowhere with her son. Daphne and Hamish asked them all in for a drink and the evening passed pleasantly although Owen, having been forced by circumstances to share the couch with Kim, hardly spoke at all.

Owen's parents stayed until late afternoon the following day. During the morning Owen took them for a drive and this time Kim insisted on staying behind to cook the lunch. Candy came back full of excitement and ice cream and sweets, having been thoroughly spoilt by her grandparents, to her father's annoyance.

Owen's mother kissed Kim affectionately as they left. His father shook her warmly by the hand. Candy hugged them and clung to them and promised to write and tell them all about her friends, especially Kim.

When they had gone, Candy wandered round deflated, following Kim wherever she went. She did not dare to go near her father – he was in such an irritable mood. She went to bed early, exhausted by the excitement of the past two days.

The peace was welcome after the noise and bustle of the weekend. Kim was tidying the kitchen before going up to her bedroom to write some letters, when Owen appeared at the door. He leaned against it, arms folded, expression cynical.

"Well, Miss Paton, judging by your behaviour while they were here, it seemed you enjoyed my parents' visit."

"Yes, thank you, Mr. Lang."

"They seemed to appreciate your company, too – as one of the family, of course." She tried to close her ears to his sarcasm. "I noticed the way you ingratiated yourself with them – making up to your future in-laws, no doubt."

This was the end. Kim flung the duster on to the floor, pushed past him as he blocked the doorway and raced up the stairs. She tugged out her suitcases, and proceeded to fill them with whatever she could lay her hands on. She flung the items in without any thought of packing them properly. In fact, she couldn't see for tears. She had to get away from him. He was breaking her heart and she felt almost ill with misery. She was so distressed she was hardly conscious of what she was doing.

She heard him mounting the stairs and rushed to close the door, but his foot got there first. He pushed against her and won the battle easily. He walked in.

"What are you doing?"

155

"Packing my cases. What else does it look like? I'm not putting up with you any longer. I've never met anyone who's so ungrateful, so uncivil and so ungentlemanly –"

He flared like a pile of paper with a lighted match thrown into it. "Ungentlemanly, did you say?" He walked towards her, menace in every stride. "*Ungentlemanly?*" He took her shoulders and swung her round to face him. "That's just about the last straw. I've taken a lot from you, Miss Paton, since you set foot in my house weeks, no, aeons ago. I've taken rank disobedience, flouting of my instructions, unpardonable rudeness. You've answered me back in such terms that if any of my subordinates at my place of work had dared to speak to me as you have done, they would have been dismissed on the spot." His fingers were bruising her flesh. "You defied me while my girl-friend was here. You were cheeky while my parents were here, and now they've gone, you're still at it. And all the time I've held back and let you get away with it. And now you dare to call me *ungentlemanly*! All right, you've accused me of it, so I'll demonstrate just how ungentlemanly I can be!"

He gripped her body and jerked her against him. "This is what a non-gentleman does to a woman – he takes advantage of her lesser strength and uses his superior muscle power to force her to do what he wants. And no matter how much she struggles – as you are doing at the moment – he always wins."

His kiss was pitiless, prolonged and totally single-minded in its purpose – to overcome her resistance and make her yield. He used every weapon, every means of persuasion at his disposal to bring about her surrender, and as he felt her body capitulate and acquiesce at last, thus admitting unreservedly that he had won, he let her go. He did it so unexpectedly that she staggered and fell backwards on to the bed.

He stood over her, hands on hips, breathing deeply, the light of victory in his eys. Now she was afraid – afraid that if he so much as laid a finger on her again, she would be utterly powerless, and worse, quite unwilling to resist whatever demands he might care to make on her.

He misinterpreted the fear in her eyes. "Don't worry, my

sweet one," even now the sarcasm was there, "I won't pursue my advantage. Rape is something I would not inflict on any woman – *however great the temptation!*" He left her.

She lay there in a stupor. It grew dark and still she did not move. When she heard vague sounds on the landing indicating that her employer was going to bed, she roused herself and unpacked her cases. Then she went to bed herself, but not to sleep.

Now things were worse than ever. After what had happened, how could she stay in his house? Yet, because of Candy, how could she go? How could she pretend that nothing was different, when everything was different?

If only another job would come along. Whatever it was, she would take it. Anything to get away. But, she asked herself over and over again – what about Candy?

CHAPTER IX

KIM slept at last. But when her alarm woke her at the usual time and she struggled back to consciousness, she wondered with dread how Owen would react to seeing her at breakfast. But she need not have worried. After a swift, half-interested glance at her, he disappeared as usual behind his newspaper. It was left to Candy to keep the conversation going until her father left for work.

That day, Kim's car misbehaved. It functioned normally when she dropped Candy outside the school, but when she tried to start the engine to collect Candy that afternoon, it would not fire. She flicked through the instruction manual and touched wires and plugs around the engine, then tried again. This time it started, with reluctance, and while she waited for Candy outside the school, she kept the engine running.

The car got them home, but Kim knew it would have to be serviced. It was over six months since she had had it looked over. But if she had to part with it for a day or two, she wondered how she would manage to get the shopping and ferry Candy to and from school.

She told Candy she would probably have to walk next day and explained why. Candy said brightly, "You can have my daddy's car and he can get a bus to work."

Kim laughed at the picture of Owen hanging around at a bus stop, clutching his briefcase and stamping his feet impatiently at the delay.

"Can't be done, Candy," she said, but she had reckoned without Candy.

That evening she said to her father, "Kim's going to have your car tomorrow, Daddy. Her car's gone wrong."

He flung down the letter he was reading. "*What did you say?*"

"Mr. Lang, before you get violent, please let me say it was

158

not my idea."

"No? You expect me to believe you didn't feed the thought into her ear with your usual subtlety?"

"No, I did *not*!" His raised eyebrows reminded her that she had forgotten her place again and her tone became more docile as she added, "I merely told her my car needed servicing and she would unfortunately have to walk to and from school tomorrow."

He snorted, picking up his letter, "Do her good for once. You spoil her by shunting her there and back as it is."

"Daddy," came a pleading voice, "Kim has lots of shopping to do tomorrow. And," she elaborated ingeniously, "shopping's heavy, isn't it? She'll have to have a car, won't she?"

He put down his letter again, this time with deliberation. He looked at Kim with a sardonic smile. "And now you're going to tell me you didn't feed that into her, and that she thought that one up herself."

"Yes, she did, Mr. Lang. Look, will you believe me when I say I don't want the use of your car, and that even if I did, I wouldn't dream of asking you for it? Anyway, I wouldn't know how to drive it, would I?"

"Too true you wouldn't." He appeared to become absorbed in his letter. Then he surfaced again. "Is it true you have a lot of shopping to get?"

"Yes, but I can go by bus."

His eyes returned to the letter, but it seemed his thoughts did not. "It could be arranged that you have my car, if it's really vital that you have one."

Her heart leapt at such a concession. His daughter applauded loud and long. She flung her arms round his neck. "I knew I had a lovely daddy!"

"My word," he murmured, taking her onslaught of affection surprisingly well, "what a show of cupboard love!" He looked at Kim with difficulty over his daughter's head – Candy was busy trying to smother his cheek with kisses – and said, "You'd better come out with me this evening for a lesson. It's a very different car from yours, much bigger for a start, and I don't want it smashed up because of mishandling by you."

Kim, still dumbfounded, said, "That's very kind of you, Mr. Lang."

He raised an eyebrow. "Is it?" was all he said.

When Kim took Candy next door, Daphne raised both eyebrows. "My dear, what goes on?"

"It's Kim's car," Candy explained seriously. "It's gone wrong."

"It's got to be serviced," Kim told her, "and Candy persuaded her father to let me borrow his." She lowered her voice. "I'm as astonished as you, Daphne. But I'm not asking 'why?' I'm just saying, 'yes, please!' "

As Kim left, Daphne told her, "If necessary, I'll put Candy to bed."

"Oh, we won't be out that long."

Daphne looked. "You never know, dear. There's always the old dodge — you might run out of petrol!"

"No." Kim shook her head. "Owen isn't like that."

"Isn't he?" murmured Daphne enigmatically. "He's as human as the rest of them, dear."

"And well I know it," Kim thought, with bitter-sweet memories of the previous evening.

Candy reached up and kissed Kim and whispered in her ear, "Are you going out with my daddy?"

"Yes, darling," Kim whispered back, deeply moved by the hope in the big blue eyes. How could she say to his child, "I'm going out with him, but it doesn't mean a thing, so please, *please* don't look like that!"

Kim slid into the driving seat of Owen's car and saw with relief that his smile was amused and a little indulgent. She got the feel of the steering wheel and controls as he explained them to her.

"It's so much bigger than mine, it frightens me," she commented, turning her head and smiling at him.

"Which is precisely why," he answered dryly, "you're going to have a lesson in driving it. So come on, get moving, and remember I'm here beside you in any emergency."

"If only," she thought as she released the handbrake and propelled the car the first few yards along the road, "those words were as prophetic as they sound!"

She drove slowly at first then, gaining courage, felt with pleasure the thrust of the engine which responded swiftly to her touch. She drove faster and he commented, "I don't think you realise just how much power you have at your disposal under that right foot of yours, so go easy, Kim."

She nodded and slowed down as she negotiated the winding, twisting country roads. After a while he said, "I think you deserve a rest. You've done well. Can I buy you a drink, Kim?"

The question made her right foot ease up so jerkily he put out a cautionary hand. "Sorry," she muttered.

He said with mock-anguish, "My poor car!"

"A drink?" she echoed. "Well, that would be nice." What else could she say? she asked herself. She couldn't tell him, "It would be wonderful to have a drink, to share *anything* with you, Owen."

He leaned forward. "We're approaching a pub now. Turn into the car park. Careful now.

She eased the car off the road and parked it neatly between two others. He patted her hand as it rested on the steering wheel.

"Very good. Yes, you can borrow my car tomorrow, provided you take me to work in it and collect me in the evening."

She looked at him, full of gratitude. "With pleasure," she said, and his eyes dwelt on hers for a few seconds before drawing away.

He ordered sherry for Kim and a beer for himself and they sat in a quiet corner near the window. It was growing dark and the lights round the walls were turned on, shedding an orange glow over the furniture and the customers. There was chatter and laughter all round them, people happy in their conviviality, taking gulps or sips from their glasses and dabbing at their mouths with handkerchiefs or the backs of their hands according to their social customs or ingrained habits.

"You drive well, Kim," Owen said suddenly. "Who taught you?"

"I had lessons," she answered, on her guard.

"Does your father drive?" She nodded. He said, with surprise, "He has a car? He can afford to run one?"

"Yes, he – he has a car."

"Your mother?"

"She drives, too." She held her breath waiting for the question, "Has she a car?" but it didn't come.

He seemed a little puzzled, so she added, hoping it would still his doubts, "Don't forget my mother goes out to work, too."

"Your brother," he said after a while, "does he live at home?"

When would the questions stop? "No." She refused to elaborate. The questions were getting too probing and therefore, dangerous. She wished she could abandon the masquerade. She remembered the words of the poet, *"To begin with, take warning, I am surely far different from what you suppose"*, and she wanted to lower her barriers and let the truth come tumbling out, like water pouring through lock-gates.

He stopped his interrogation and asked, searching in his pockets for a cigarette, "Is that drink to your liking?"

She fiddled with her bracelet – the one he had given her. "It's fine, thanks, Mr. Lang."

He held up the cigarette and asked, "Do you object if I smoke?" She shook her head.

"Don't you think," he murmured, drawing the cigarette to life with his lighter, "you could abandon etiquette and call me by my first name? You call me Owen to the neighbours, you call me Owen to my mother –"

"How do you know?"

"I heard you. So why not call me Owen to my face?"

She smiled shyly. "Yes, Owen."

"My word, what timidity suddenly!" He waved away the smoke around him and leaned back, contemplating her. "Obviously the treatment I meted out last night had a profound effect on your behaviour towards me." She smiled. "I'd better do it more often, if it's going to make you so tractable and obedient."

She coloured deeply and he watched the process with almost scientific interest, which made her feel even more embarrassed. He laughed.

"Don't you think, Owen," she said desperately trying to distract his attention, "we should go?"

"No. I'm quite happy where I am, quite satisfied with the company I'm keeping."

"But Candy —"

"Daphne will put her to bed." Still she fidgeted and he clasped his hand over hers. "Look, she's my child. I'm not worried, so why should you be?"

She sighed and had to be content. "You're the boss, I suppose, so —"

"I certainly am." His hand squeezed hers. "And don't you forget it."

He leaned forward, elbow on the table, cigarette smouldering between his fingers, his other hand still covering hers. Idly he looked round at the other customers, at the people coming and going. Now and then their eyes met and they would smile at each other. How long, Kim wondered in a dream, could this harmony, this accord between them, go on?

"*Do you suppose,*" the poet had asked, "*you will find in me your ideal? Do you think the friendship of me would be unalloy'd satisfaction?*" "Yes," Kim wanted to cry in answer, "yes, yes!"

"I'll drive back," he said, stubbing out his cigarette and rising. "It's dark now."

They went through the swing doors and into the chill of the evening air. He found her hand in the darkness and they walked round the back to the car park. He let her into the car and as they drove home he told her,

"In the morning I'll take your car along to my garage first thing and get them to service it. It should only take them a day. Then I'll get one of the mechanics to give me a lift back home — it's not far and they're very good that way — and you can take Candy to school and run me on to work. All right?" He sought her eyes swiftly in the dimness.

"It's very good of you to go to so much trouble."

He laughed. "Anything to oblige a lady who's also such an

efficient housekeeper."

She was still wondering about the incredible change in his attitude when he turned the car into the drive. He was being so pleasant, so agreeable she could not understand it.

In the hall he asked, "What are you going to do now?"

She shrugged. "Go upstairs, read, go to bed."

"I see." He thought for a moment, appeared to hesitate, began to speak but changed his mind. He lifted his arm and rested it for a few moments across her shoulders. "Well, goodnight, Kim."

Unreasonably disappointed, she replied, "Goodnight, Owen. Thank you for this evening."

He nodded. He did not leave the foot of the stairs until she had disappeared into her bedroom.

Next morning everything went according to plan. Owen, returning from the garage, told her, "Your car will be ready this afternoon. They offered to deliver it and leave it outside if you're not in, so I accepted."

She thanked him. "What about paying?"

"Oh, don't worry, they'll send the bill to you. Did you think I'd offer to pay it?" He smiled provocatively. "But you never know, with a little – er – persuasion – of the right sort, of course, I might even offer to do that."

"No, thanks," she said, smiling but avoiding his eyes.

"You disappoint me," he murmured as they walked to the car to find an impatient Candy jumping about in the back seat.

Kim drove to the school where they left her skipping happily – Kim thought, a little more happily than usual – through the school gates. Then she ran Owen to work, moving slowly along the drive to the building in which he worked. As he opened the car door, he glanced around at all the other cars driving up and depositing the man of the family.

"You see," he said wickedly, "you're doing your wifely duty, just like all the other wives. Doesn't that please you? Doesn't it give you ideas?"

Before she could reply, he had gone.

Kim enjoyed shopping in Owen's car. Despite its length she managed to reverse it neatly into a narrow parking space. Owen would be proud of her, she told herself, then checked her thoughts which were becoming too possessive. She drove to the school that afternoon and Candy swaggered across the road, drawing as much attention as possible to her father's large car – and to the fact that Kim was driving it – by waving ostentatiously to all her friends. There were a few raised eyebrows among the mothers, too.

When it was time for Kim to collect Owen, Candy went with her. The man at the gate, recognising Owen's car, lifted his hand in a surprised salute and Kim swept grandly up the drive, feeling important. She waited where Owen had indicated and as the time moved on, Candy grew fidgety. She wound down the window, wound it back, tried to fiddle with the controls until Kim had to reprimand her. Then Candy became irritable and said, opening the door, "I'm going to find my daddy. I know where his office is."

She was out and through the swing doors before Kim could stop her. Hurriedly she locked the car and chased into the building looking right and left. She caught sight of a small figure disappearing into an office along the corridor and raced after her, intending to pull her back.

"What the blazes," said an astonished voice, "are you two doing here?"

"You're late, Daddy," Candy said, coolly, "so we came to find you."

"*I* didn't," Kim snapped, "I came to find *you*." She tugged at Candy's hand. "Come back to the car."

"Oh, let her stay. You, too. There's something I must finish before I leave for home. Sit down somewhere and be quiet, both of you."

But Candy dashed back into the corridor, being unusually disobedient, and Kim ran after her.

"Well," said another astonished voice, "look who's here!"

"Marvin!" Kim retreated into Owen's room and Candy made a dive for cover behind her father, her dislike for Marvin making her afraid.

"Hall*o*, sweetie," Marvin said to Kim. "What a pleasant surprise!" He followed her into Owen's office and looked her up and down. "Charming as ever. Isn't it time we became re-acquainted?"

Kim glanced at Owen, who was frowning.

"Look, Ward, if you want to make a date with my house-keeper, do it outside my office, will you?"

Marvin shrugged and followed Kim into the corridor, leaving Owen's door ajar. "Sorry to appear to have neglected you, Kim," Marvin said, "but as I told you, my hours are uncertain. I have time off only when work allows. However," he picked up her hand and played with her fingers, "this even-ing is definitely available. What do you say, sweetie? Dinner and dance?"

"Well, Marvin. I –"

Owen appeared at his door. "How the devil can I concen-trate with you two drooling over each other out here?"

"We're being moved on, darling," said Marvin, grinning. "There's an empty room along the corridor. Come in there, then we won't be disturbed."

Owen gave them a filthy look and slammed his door. With reluctance, Kim followed Marvin into the other room.

"Now, what's your answer?" he asked as soon as the door was closed.

"No, thanks."

"Now, now," he held up a warning hand. "If you refuse to come out with me, sweetie, you know what I'll do. I'll tell dear Owen all."

With satisfaction he watched anxiety crease Kim's face into a worried frown. "That's blackmail," she blurted out.

"Yes, it is, isn't it? But you know what I said – fair means or foul. And I'm as good as my word, darling, I promise you."

She saw the malice in his smile. Yes, he was quite capable of doing what he had threatened. She could not let that hap-pen now, not when relations between her and Owen had im-proved so much, and he even seemed to be liking her a little.

She eyed the door. Hoping to avoid having to give an immediate answer, she wrenched at the handle and pulled, dived into the corridor managing to evade Marvin's hand. She raced to Owen's room, thrust open the door and saw Berenice looking cool and charming in a long white lab. coat bending down so near to Owen that their cheeks were almost touching.

"Yes, but Owen," she was saying in her deep husky voice, "don't you think –?"

She stopped and looked up, astonished at Kim's precipitate arrival. Owen saw Kim's flushed face, heard her deep breaths, saw Marvin looking irritable in the doorway, and smiled broadly.

"Unusual for you, Ward, to have to do the chasing, isn't it?"

Marvin ignored the sarcasm. "Well, Kim, what's the answer? Or do I –?"

Hastily Kim said, "Yes, yes, this evening. Seven-thirty?"

Grinning now that he had got his own way, Marvin nodded. "On the dot." He raised a triumphant hand to Owen, to whom he said, "I'm off now. See you tomorrow." He watched gloating, as ill-humour nudged Owen's smile out of the way.

When Marvin had gone, Owen motioned Kim to the chair next to Candy's. "Having interrupted us, you'll have to be patient a bit longer. Now, Berenice ..." As they discussed an intricate technical point, Berenice revealed a scientific knowledge which left Kim dazzled and envious. She thought, "She has so much – beauty, intelligence, the ability to talk to Owen in his own language, the language of the scientist." With all those assets, she would make him an excellent wife ... Restlessly, Kim rose and wandered to the window, ignoring Owen's irritable tutting.

"Shall we go into my room, Owen?" Berenice asked softly. "We won't be interrupted there, I can guarantee that."

"No. We'll leave it for the moment." He glanced at his watch. "Are you free this evening, Berenice? Could you come over to my place, then we can continue our discussion in pleasant surroundings and," he looked pointedly at Kim, "a quiet house with my daughter in bed and no one else around to

167

interrupt –"

"Wonderful, darling," Berenice breathed, looking at Kim to see how she was taking the endearment that had slipped so easily from her inviting lips.

Kim did not react at all, but Owen smiled warmly at the woman at his side. "Then," he added, looking deliberately at his housekeeper, but talking to Berenice, "I could take you out for a drink."

Berenice's smile was full of promise.

"Shall we wait in the car, Mr. Lang?" Kim asked stiffly. So he was taking another woman for a drink this evening. Well, he would get more out of Berenice in return for his expenditure of money than he had from her. Berenice left, murmuring, "Till later, Owen."

"I'm coming now, Miss Paton," he said with irritation, collecting books and papers and stuffing them into his briefcase. They would not all go in, so without a word he handed Kim a pile of books.

She took them awkwardly in her arms, calling to Candy and making for the entrance doors.

"I'm driving, Miss Paton," Owen snapped.

Relations back to normal, Kim thought with a sinking heart. She let Candy into the back of the car and got in beside her. Owen did not comment on her choice of seat. He did not even appear to notice.

As they swung round into the sideway, Kim remarked that the garage had kept their word and had returned her car. She saw it with a rush of affection and relief. Now she would not be under an obligation to her employer to provide her with transport.

Still clutching the pile of books and with Owen coming to stand impatiently behind her, she found the key and opened the front door. As she stepped inside, Candy rushed past making for the stairs and the pile of books went flying out of Kim's arms and slithered along the hall floor.

"Oh, for heaven's sake!" muttered Owen, bending down beside her and picking them up.

Kim stretched forward to get hold of a particularly large

...ne and noted its name as she placed it on top of the pile which had collected on the floor. She saw the author's name too and said spontaneously and with filial pleasure, "My father's book!"

Owen stared at her and stood up. "What did you say?"

She rose and repeated, "My —" saw his astonishment and came to her senses. She took a breath, tried to retract. "Nothing, Mr. Lang. I didn't say anything. Really I didn't."

He took the book from the pile on the floor. He looked at the name on the binding, opened the cover and stared at the name inside. He read aloud, "Aldous Paton, Ph.D., M.Sc., F.R.I.C., Professor of Physical Chemistry at —" He named the university. "This is your *father*?"

She did not answer.

"Your father," he persisted, "is a university professor? Your father is a scientist, a distinguished scientist, author of a number of textbooks and author of this book, an important standard work on the subject?"

Still avoiding his eyes, she nodded. His lips tightened.

"Come into the sitting-room, Miss Paton." He picked up his briefcase. "Bring that pile of books with you."

"But the meal, Mr. Lang, I must get the meal . . ."

"Damn the meal!" came the emphatic answer. "You and I are going to talk."

"Yes, Mr. Lang." Docile now — in her present precarious position, how could she be otherwise? — she followed him into the sitting-room.

He dumped his briefcase on the couch, took the books from Kim's arms and threw them down beside it, thrust his hands into his pockets and said, "Now. Let's get this straight. Your father is not — as I in my innocence, and as a direct consequence of your deliberate misrepresentation, imagined — a financially embarrassed working man, living in semi-poverty. Your mother is not an overworked and harassed housewife, driven to finding a job to eke out the family finances. You were not a 'burden' to them because you were forced to live at home, without a job, bringing in no income —" He thumped the back of the armchair. "In fact, the truth is that your father

169

holds a position of esteem in the university world, is earning a sizeable salary and provides his family with a civilized, comfortable home with no suggestion whatsoever of being unable to support them – *without financial assistance from his daughter!*"

She looked down at her clasped hands, feeling as humiliated as a child being reprimanded by a teacher in front of the class.

He sat down. He did not invite her to do the same. He selected a cigarette. "Tell me," he went on, lighting it and expelling the smoke, "*does* your mother 'go out to work' as you put it?"

Her answer was barely audible. "She's a teacher of chemistry at a large comprehensive school."

"And your brother?"

"A lecturer in chemistry at a polytechnic."

"So. You come from a family of scientists, the breed you so despise." He laughed, but there was no joy in it. "And you came to work for one of the same kind, another scientist! The irony of it really gets me." He regarded her thoughtfully. "Tell me, with all that brain-power in the family, how is it you missed out on your education?"

She should have known the question was inevitable and should have been prepared. But she floundered in her reply. "I – I was the – er – the odd one out. I didn't – quite – make the grade. In the eyes of my father, I was a failure."

Well, she tried to justify her remark to herself, that was true, wasn't it? His attitude to arts graduates was the same as Owen's – he thought them irrelevant to this modern day and age, as he had said repeatedly in the past.

"So," her employer probed again, "you got nowhere in the educational stakes? You've got nothing to offer except your housekeeping potential?"

She skirted round the question giving a truthful, if not a complete, answer. "I did a secretarial course."

"Did you indeed?" He eyed her reflectively. "That's useful to know. If in future I need some letters typed at home, instead of picking it out with one finger on my portable typewriter, I can get you to do it – for *extra money*, of course."

She knew his emphasis was intentional, reminding her of

his generous gesture in increasing her salary when she had started to work for him.

"That extra money you gave me for my parents, I'll pay it back, Mr. Lang. I accepted it under false pretences, so I'll give it back, all of it. I've got the money in the bank. In fact, I'll write out a cheque now, if you'll wait until I get my handbag."

"And how were you intending to work out the exact sum you would have to repay?"

"Well, I'd – er – add up the extra amount you added to my wages and deduct it –"

"Don't be any more stupid than you can help, Miss Paton."

She recognised the insult but could not retaliate. Having given such a poor picture of her own abilities, she felt she had asked for it.

"Keep the money." He settled more comfortably in his chair and, by his expression, she guessed he was all set to provoke. "So there's nothing in that head of yours after all. Beautiful but brainless. It's a pity it always happens that way – there's a sort of law about it. All housekeepers are the same. It's as well I made up my mind early never to marry one." When would he stop his taunting? "I began to wonder, that evening I caught you reading Walt Whitman and saw all those erudite books on your bookshelf, if I was wrong about your intellectual ability, but it seems that, clever though your family is, you didn't inherit the family brains. As I suspected, all those books were a façade, a pretence designed to fool me into thinking you were intelligent." He paused. "Weren't they?"

She eyed him suspiciously. Was that a statement, or a question, designed to force the truth from her? Whatever it was, she knew she must remain silent. She had to maintain this appearance of being dull and obtuse. He went on looking at her.

She murmured, "I'm sorry about the lies, Mr. Lang."

He stubbed out his cigarette and rose. "I should think you are. From the start, you've been one gigantic untruth. Slowly, slowly, and one by one," his tone grew insinuating, "those veils are being peeled off. If you stay here long enough," his eyes held a wicked gleam of anticipation, "we'll get down to the bare essentials, to the real you."

She coloured at his meaning. "Are you going to let me stay, Mr. Lang?"

"Why? Do you expect me to get rid of you just because I've discovered you have a famous father and an accomplished mother and brother? Now you're being stupid again, but I'll make allowances. I know you can't help it. But," he approached her, slowly, lazily and stood, hands in pockets, watching her closely, "there must be no more falsehoods, no more lies. Otherwise, my beautiful but dumb young woman, I shall be looking for another housekeeper and you for another job. Is that clear?" She nodded. He looked at the clock on the mantelpiece. "Now, if your boy-friend is coming, and my girl-friend is coming, we'd better get on with our meal. And my daughter will be shouting to be fed. Where is she, by the way?"

"Upstairs, probably reading a comic."

"Thank heaven for comics," muttered her father. "Nonsense most of them, but at least they keep the kids quiet and give us adults a bit of peace."

She went into the kitchen. Peace? she thought. She would know no peace now. If the last "veil" should be torn down, the last lie disclosed, then Candy or no Candy, she, Kim Paton, would be bundled back to the bosom of her family and became once again a member of the "great unemployed".

Berenice arrived, dressed for an evening of pleasure, not business. She looked, as usual, cool and beautiful, her hard eyes filled with condescension for Kim's lowly place in the household.

If only, Kim thought vindictively, I could tell her, just once, that I'm a graduate too, that I'm not the ignoramus she thinks I am.

Before Marvin came, Kim settled Candy down. Candy asked hopefully, 'Are you going out with my daddy again?'

"No, darling."

"Who, then? The man I don't like?" Kim nodded. "Stay at home, Kim. Don't go with him." There was desperation in her voice, betraying some kind of premonition inside her which told her that Marvin could only bring trouble and unhappiness to the house.

"Don't worry," Kim kissed Candy's forehead gently, "I'll be all right, I promise."

But as she closed the bedroom door, she acknowledged that Candy's uneasiness had communicated itself to her and anxiety nibbled at her like a mouse at a piece of cheese.

Marvin, when he saw her, let out a long loud wolf-whistle. She did not think she merited such flattery, having taken the minimum of pains with her appearance, and thought he was only doing it to provoke Owen.

That Owen was provoked was plain, judging by the icy glare that came her way from his sub-zero eyes. *He* had no praise for how she looked. But, she thought, as she returned his stare with a carelessly amused one of her own – she secretly congratulated herself on her new-found acting ability – it didn't matter what he thought, did it? She was not going out with him.

Marvin took her dining and dancing as he had promised. The evening passed without a spark of real enjoyment on Kim's part. Marvin had a look of purpose in his eyes, like someone with an objective in view. To him, she was sure, the evening spent together was only a preliminary, a means to an end. She knew that she would have to use all the guile, all the cunning at her disposal to get herself out of trouble before the evening was over.

When she suggested they should go, he did not object. "Owen will almost certainly be out," she explained. "He invited Berenice to the house to finish some work," here Marvin laughed cynically, "and then he promised to take her out for a drink."

"So the house will be empty?"

"Well, Candy will be there, but in bed. Daphne will go in now and then to make sure she's all right."

"But when you get back, presumably she won't?"

"No." It did not occur to her to wonder where his questions might be leading.

He took her home. It was not until they stepped into the house and he pulled her close that she chided herself for being so dull-witted. Of course he had been eager to bring her home. Without thinking, she had given him the information he desired – that Owen would be out with his girl-friend. How could she have been so naïve? She tried to break free of him, but she might have been pitting her strength against that of a polar bear for all the use it was. He forced her into the sitting-room and closed the door.

CHAPTER X

MARVIN propelled her backwards towards the couch and pushed her down. She gasped, "No, Marvin, no!" but he was deaf to her plea. He dropped to the couch beside her and pulled her into his arms.

A key turned in the lock. With a curse, Marvin thrust her away. He stood up, uncertain now. Kim smoothed her hair and straightened her dress. "Owen's back," she said. "You'll have to leave."

"I'm damned if I'm going to let him spoil my fun." He seized her hand and jerked her up. "Come on, into my car."

She tried to twist her hand from his, but he held it fast. They passed Owen in the hall. His look told Kim exactly what he thought of her. She opened her mouth to plead with him, but Marvin pulled her behind him and out of the front door.

Still gripping her hand, he searched for his car keys and opened the door. "Get in!" he hissed, but she pulled away from him.

"Do as I say, and stop resisting, or I'll —"

She gave a mighty tug and managed to free her hand. She turned to run, but he pulled her backwards by the shoulders and she stumbled against him. "Don't, Marvin," she pleaded.

He wrenched her round and raised his hand when a cool, hard voice said, "I shouldn't, if I were you, Ward. It's not a good idea to maltreat your boss's housekeeper. It could affect your promotion prospects, among other things."

Marvin uttered a loud curse and Kim shut her eyes, waiting for him to denounce her to her employer. It did not come. Instead, Marvin slammed into his car and drove away.

Kim swayed and Owen's arm came round her to lead her back to the house. He closed the front door and she stood in the hall, shaking with reaction and relief.

175

"For a woman who once boasted of her prowess in handling men," Owen rasped, "you were having to put up an unbelievably hard struggle in defence of your virtue."

She could not answer.

"Why are you shaking like this? Are you really as upset as you appear to be, or are you playing on my sympathies and trying to make me feel protective towards you?"

She shook her head. "I'm s-sorry. Th-thank you for h-helping me."

His arm went round her again and he took her into his sitting-room. "Sit down. You need a drink." As he handed it to her, he said, casually, cynically, "You were 'handling' him as well as you 'handled' me in your bedroom, weren't you?" She sipped the drink. She supposed that once again she had asked for it and, with his usual ruthlessness, he was giving it to her. "It was a good thing for you my name wasn't Marvin Ward the other night, wasn't it? And it was lucky for you this evening that Berenice wanted to get home early. Otherwise, I hate to think what would have happened to our chaste little Kim Paton." He helped himself to a drink. "I told you, didn't I, that Ward meant what he said about 'getting' you, come what may. He may not have succeeded yet – although he got near to it tonight – but I'm warning you, if you go out with him once more, my girl, you've had it. And to be crude, which unfortunately I have to be to make you see reason, so will he."

"Don't worry," she whispered, finishing her drink, "there won't be a 'next time.' "

"I should hope not." His voice was softer now. "Feeling better?"

She smiled up at him, but it was an uncertain, wavering smile. He caught her hand and pulled her up. His hands rested on her shoulders. His gaze moved over her face, contemplated her eyes, her chin and settled on her mouth. Her heart throbbed like a drumbeat as she wondered, "Will he kiss me?" But he took his hands away and wandered to the fireplace, standing with his back to her, raking in his pocket for a cigarette.

"You'd better go, Kim. You look all in."

"Yes, Mr. Lang."

"Owen," he corrected.

"Yes, Owen," she said obediently, and he turned and smiled. "Goodnight, Owen."

He nodded, still smiling, and she went upstairs.

When the telephone rang the following evening, Kim was in her bedroom, reading. Owen answered the call.

"Yes," she heard him say, "this is Owen Lang speaking. Who is that?" He listened. "Oh, hallo!" He seemed pleased to hear the caller's name.

Berenice, Kim thought with disgust, and subsided into her book. He must have chatted to her for some time, for the murmur of his voice went on and on. Then it rose slightly. "Yes, she's upstairs."

He's talking to Berenice about me? Kim thought unbelievingly.

"I know," Owen was saying, "she told me all about you. I had a copy of your husband's book –"

My mother! she thought, astonished, he's talking to my mother!

She flung her book on to the bed and chased down the stairs, stopping near the bottom as Owen turned his back and draped himself against the staircase as if unwilling to hand over to her.

So, impatient now, Kim sat on the stairs and fretted while the conversation went on.

"I understand," her employer said, "we're scientists one and all, your daughter excepted." A pause, then a quick glance round at the girl in question. "Yes, she told me, but it was purely accidental – she let it out when she saw my copy of her father's book." Kim heard her mother laugh and he laughed with her. He said, "I'll hand you over to her now. She's almost pawing the ground with impatience! Yes, nice to have had a chat." He listened. "I'd love to meet you all some time – I'd be delighted to have a talk with your distinguished husband!"

Kim snatched the phone from Owen, but he lingered in the hall. "Hallo, Mum. What?" She looked at Owen and answered with doubt in her voice, "Yes, I suppose he is."

He whispered in her ear, "He is what?"

She covered the mouthpiece. "Charming, my mother said."

He grinned at her, "It's plain you don't agree," and went into the dining-room, leaving the door ajar.

"Sorry, Mum, what were you saying?"

"I was saying, dear, that I've heard of a marvellous job for you. A colleague of mine at school knows an author who's looking for someone – preferably a graduate, so you would qualify – to do some research for him. He's writing a book on the origins of English drama – you know, historical stuff – and I thought it would be just right for you. How about it, darling?"

"But, Mum," she lowered her voice, "how can I?"

"You're thinking of the little girl, I suppose? Darling, you can't sacrifice the rest of your life to looking after someone else's child, however fond of her you may be. It would be a shocking waste of your university education, for a start."

"But, Mum," her voice was tight in her throat, "I – I just don't see how –" If only she could tell her mother the truth, that it was not only the child she loved, it was the father, too, and that if she left she would never see him again and she would then be only half alive.

"Kim," her mother urged, "the break has got to come. You can't shut your eyes to it. You're just an employee, dear, remember that, nothing more, nothing less. If he wants a woman to look after his daughter permanently, he'll just have to marry again."

"Oh, Mum!" The tears were spilling over now and were reflected in her voice.

"Darling," her mother's words were an urgent whisper, "make the break swift and fast, the quicker the better. You know, like ripping a piece of plaster off a wound. Do it suddenly, then it doesn't hurt so much, either you or her."

"Mum," her voice was so low it was barely audible, "can I think about it?"

178

"Only a few days, dear. You can't afford to delay. This is a wonderful opportunity and you know how many people there are in your line, fully qualified, all looking for suitable jobs. It will be snapped up, Kim."

"All right, Mum. Thanks for telling me. Just give me a day or two, then I'll let you know. It will probably be 'yes'."

"Darling, that's wonderful, but hurry, won't you? 'Bye for now. Regards to your Mr. Lang. Take care of yourself."

" 'Bye, Mum." She lowered the receiver on to the cradle and stood for a moment staring at it, tears dampening her cheeks. "*My* Mr. Lang! The irony of it!" she thought.

So the end was in sight.

"Bad news, Kim?" He was beside her, looking anxious.

"No, no." She drew in her breath to check a sob and made for the stairs, taking them two at a time to get away from his questions.

Kim and Candy and Sue, Candy's friend, were picnicking by the lake. Kim had packed sandwiches and cakes and had met them outside the school. Now they had eaten and the remaining food had been put away. Candy and Sue were paddling.

Kim lay back and relaxed under the trees, listening to the repetitive and beautiful song of a thrush overhead. She wondered if Owen was enjoying his day in London. She doubted it. He had not been enthusiastic about the all-day conference he had been invited to attend.

"I won't be back until late," he had told her. "I shall have my evening meal in town."

She had not come to a decision about the job her mother had told her about. She had argued with herself until her brain had rebelled and closed down, refusing to perform and provide the answer, like a computer that had gone wrong.

Now, lying under the trees, she tried to be rational. It was the sort of work she had dreamed about ever since she had got her degree. She had only taken this housekeeping job, she reasoned, doing her utmost now to shut out the thrush repeating itself so ardently above her head, as a fill-in, until a more suitable one came along. But in her calculations she hadn't allowed for falling in love with her employer.

Candy and Sue were talking. In the still air, their voices carried. "She's not really your mummy," Sue was saying cruelly.

"She is!"

"She *isn't*, Candy. My mummy says she should be, because she lives with your daddy."

Kim turned over on to her front and put her hand to her head. Is that what the mothers were saying? The thrush flew away with a flutter of wings.

"But," persisted Sue relentlessly, "my daddy works at the same place as your daddy, and he says your daddy's going to marry another lady called Berry something."

"Yes, I know, Berry-niece," Candy said. "But he's not, he's *not* going to marry her. I hate her. She's horrible. I love Kim, not her."

"If he does," went on Sue, "that Berry-something will be your mummy."

"I don't want her. I'll tell my daddy I don't want her. It's Kim who's got to be my mummy." Candy sounded near to tears.

Kim clapped her hands over her ears. How much longer could she stand it? Her mother was right. Make the break clean and swift, then it wouldn't hurt. But her mother was thinking of Candy, not of her own daughter, Kim. Kim knew that her own particular pain would hurt for the rest of her life.

She called to the children. She put on a bright face and a cheerful voice and dropped Sue at her house. Then she drove Candy home.

"Enjoyed it?" Kim asked Candy.

"Lovely!" Candy looked up at Kim, her eyes troubled and full of question, but to Kim's relief no question was asked.

Candy settled down in bed, and her goodnight kiss was more urgent than usual. Kim sat in her room, she was restless and wished Owen would come home. She thought fretfully, if she missed him so much after only a day away in town, what would it be like when he was away from her for the rest of her life?

As she took a book from the shelves, she heard the back door open and footsteps walk along the hall. Owen! she thought. He's back early. Delightedly she ran on to the landing to greet him.

But the man coming up the stairs was not Owen. It was Marvin.

She turned pale. "What do you want? You had no right to walk in uninvited."

"I came in round the back. If I'd had to wait for an invitation from you, I would have had to wait for ever, wouldn't I?"

"Owen – Owen's in," she lied, hoping to put him off. But he sent her feeble protestations flying, like a batsman hitting a ball to the boundary.

"He's not. He's in London at a conference. The whole section knows he's been away all day."

"He'll be back any minute."

"He won't. He may not be back until after midnight. These conferences go on for a long time and they often gang up afterwards and go for a meal somewhere." He urged her backwards into the bedroom. "So, my sweet, I've called to see my elusive girl-friend where we can talk without supervision or danger of being – overheard, if you get my meaning."

"Get out of my room!" She hoped belligerence would deter him. But, by the look in his eyes, it incited him instead.

"What? When I've just arrived? Later, darling, later." He sat on the chair. "Mind if I smoke, sweetie?"

"Of course I mind. The smell will linger and he'll know –"

"Yes, he will, won't he? You know, I never thought of that."

He got his cigarette going and looked her over. "We've time, plenty of time."

She sat on the bed wondering what to do. She tried appealing to him. "Marvin, please, *please* go. I know what you're after and I can tell you here and now, it's no use –"

"Isn't it?" He leaned forward, an ugly look on his face. "Listen, sweetie, I always get my man – or to paraphrase, my woman. Never failed yet. I'm an old hand."

She eyed the doorway, measuring the distance she would have to run to get through it. If she could wake Candy, get her to go for Daphne ... As he lifted his cigarette to his lips, she made a dive for the door, but he was too quick for her. He closed it and stood against it. "Don't do that again," he threatened, "or I won't waste another minute."

She sat on the bed again, pretending to yield. Anything to gain time, while she thought about what to do. She was growing frightened now. In her desperation, she even eyed the window.

He glanced at the books on the shelves. "My word, high class stuff, that. But then she is, of course, a literary type, isn't she? It's not often I get the chance to – get my way with quality, as well as beauty. It should prove a novel experience."

Desperate now, she looked at her watch, but that made things worse. It told her that Owen would not be home for hours. It was growing dark.

"I want to turn on the light." Her voice was brittle.

"I think not." He stubbed out his cigarette. "Twilight is so conducive to – surrender."

He wandered across to her, but rather than have him sitting on the bed beside her, she stood. His arms went round her and she thought it better to submit – thus far. She even let him kiss her, unpleasant though it was.

But when he began in earnest to make love to her, she pulled away and tried to struggle out of his hold. Appalled now, helpless in the tentacles that were his arms, she reproached herself for what was happening. Surely there must have been something she could have done to have prevented things from getting this far. His grip was choking her now, pressing the breath from her body ...

Through the fog that was clouding her brain bringing her thought processes almost to a standstill, she sensed the light tread of footsteps on the stairs, a raised, pleased, male voice calling her name.

"Kim? Are you there? I came back early –" There was a light, quick tap and the door opened.

Owen filled the doorway. His face, clear and bright as a day in high summer, darkened like the sky before a storm. White now with anger, his face stiff with derision and contempt, he watched her. She stood, her body taut against Marvin's, bracing herself against the pressure of his arms. She could not know that such an action, in its attempt to deny responsibility for being where she was, only set the seal on her guilt in Owen's eyes.

Marvin looked down at her, his expression full of assumed regret. "Sorry, darling," he murmured, deliberately implicating her in their apparent intrigue, "we've been interrupted. And we were getting on so well together, too."

He let her go. Kim covered her face with shaking hands.

Owen snarled, "Get out, Ward."

Marvin smoothed back his hair, straightened his tie, brushed his jacket as though it were covered with hairs from Kim's head — he even picked off an imaginary one. "You chose the wrong moment, *Mr*. Lang," he remarked, his voice even. "Just a little later and I would have achieved my object. Your housekeeper was only too willing to oblige."

"It's a lie," she choked, the tips of her fingers pressing into her cheeks. "He forced his way into the house. He came in through the kitchen –"

Marvin nodded his head at her. "That's her story. I don't blame her, because she works here. All the same, to clear myself, I must inform you that she invited me."

She flung at him, "That's a disgusting, outrageous lie!"

Owen said, quiet now, "I said get out, Ward."

"Certainly, when you've heard what I've got to say."

"Marvin," Kim whispered, "please . . ."

He ignored her. "You may not know it, old chap, but your housekeeper is a graduate, an arts graduate. She has a degree in English literature, the type you hate so much. She took this job under false pretences."

Owen asked her coldly, "Is this true?"

She nodded.

"I see." There was a weary finality about his voice. "So my hunch about your real educational background was right."

183

To Marvin he said, "Now you've done your worst, you can leave."

"Okay, boss. Happy landings, sweetie," he leered at Kim. "And the best of luck. You'll need it, chum."

They listened to the footsteps descending the stairs, heard the front door slammed shut.

Kim mumbled, her face still covered, "I'm sorry. I'm sorry about everything."

Still he said nothing, so she raised dull eyes only to recoil as the look in his shocked her. "So, while I was away in London, you asked your boy-friend to the house and invited him into your room. It didn't occur to you that I might return early, having decided – for reasons of my own – to cut out the ritual dinner and get back home."

"Mr. Lang," she implored, "you'll have to take my word, although I know you'll find it difficult to believe me after so many lies, but I didn't invite him here. He walked in. I hoped – I mean, I thought it was you and went on to the landing to meet you, but it was Marvin." But she could see she was appealing to him in vain.

"You've lied to me so consistently since the day you arrived, I can't believe you know the meaning of the word 'truth', in the moral, let alone the scientific sense. As you said about yourself in relation to your family, you're the odd one out."

"I shall have to leave, Mr. Lang," she said wearily. "The situation between us, my educational background, my lack of qualifications for the job you're employing me to do . . .'

"That reference I got about your abilities in domestic science –?"

"That, like all the other things, was false. I know you won't, you can't forgive me." She went on after a pause in which he did not refute her statement, "I told your mother about my degree, and I told Daphne."

"And your boy-friend. Everyone, in fact, except the one who should have been told – me."

"That was because of the things you had said about people like me – that you wouldn't have one in the house."

"So you were afraid that if I knew, I'd throw you out?"

"Yes."

"And you didn't want to go?" She shook her head. "Why, because of Candy?"

With her nod, she knew she was lying to him again.

She whispered, "There's no need for you to dismiss me, Mr. Lang. I'm leaving anyway. I've got the offer of a job, the sort I've been longing for — literary research. It's for an author who intends to write a book about early English drama."

"Make the break clean and swift," her mother had said.

"I'll pack tomorrow and get things in order for you, and then I'll leave the day after tomorrow." She sought his eyes. "In dismissing myself, I'm only anticipating your dismissal of me. I'd have to go anyway. You'll be marrying Berenice soon —"

"Who told you that?"

She shrugged. "I heard. It's going round your place of work."

He drummed with restless fingers on the back of a chair. "Is it, really? Who started that rumour, I wonder?" But he did not deny it, so she knew it must be true. Her heart was breaking and she was afraid it would show in her eyes. He went out, but she followed him. "I'll get you a meal, Mr. Lang."

"I'll get it myself."

She did not see him again that evening and the following morning he had breakfasted and left before she got down. She had to appear bright in front of Candy, who was bubbling over with good cheer. Kim took her to school, then went next door to Daphne.

It was then, and only then, that she allowed herself the luxury of letting her emotions take over. She put her head down on Daphne's table and cried. Daphne left her alone until she stopped.

"Don't tell me," said Daphne. "It's all up."

Kim nodded, drying her tears. "I'm leaving tomorrow."

"You mean he's thrown you out, like all the others?"

"No, I've dismissed myself, but I've only saved him the bother of doing it." She told Daphne everything.

"I think Owen had half guessed about my degree, though. It wasn't the surprise to him I thought it would be."

'So why the walk-out?"

She answered simply, "I've been offered another job – researching for an author. Much more in my line."

Daphne said, resigned, "I suppose it's for the best, in the long run, but my dear, what about Candy?"

Kim shook her head and the tears began again. But even now she could not tell Daphne about her feelings for Owen.

"Don't worry, Kim, I'll look after Candy until he gets someone else. Poor little kiddy. She's so fond of you."

Kim sobbed again, so Daphne made her some strong coffee with "a dash of something in it," she said, to help her pull herself together.

By the time Kim collected Candy from school, she had come to terms with the inevitability of it all. She had known in her heart she would have had to leave some time, only she had refused to admit it.

But, she asked herself helplessly, how should she tell Candy? "Make the break swift," her mother had said. Best not to tell Candy. Go – just like that!

"Cowardly," whispered part of her. "Sensible," whispered the other.

For the last time she settled Candy down at bedtime. She sat on the bed and Candy's arms came up and imprisoned her neck. "I'm never afraid to wake in the mornings now, Kim, in case you've gone away. I know you'll always be here, always for ever."

"Oh, Candy." Kim buried her face in Candy's hair. Candy felt the tears trickling against her cheeks.

"Your eyes are watering again, Kim, like they did once before. Mine don't water so much now, since you came."

"Don't they, darling? That's good." Kim found her handkerchief. "See? Mine are dry now. I feel better. Go to sleep, Candy. Goodnight, darling." As she closed the door, she whispered, "And goodbye."

She called in to see Hamish. He patted her on the back. "Don't take it too hard. You're well rid of the brute, Kim." And to his astonishment Kim burst into tears. "For heaven's sake, what have I said?"

Daphne raised her eyebrows at her husband, who did likewise to her. "No!" he whispered to his wife.

"Could be," Daphne whispered back. "Kim," she said aloud, "it's best this way."

"Clean break and all that," muttered her husband.

"And," Daphne promised, "I'll pacify Candy. And, if necessary, her father."

When Kim left them, she went upstairs to tidy herself and to finish her packing. She put all her books into a box and loaded them into the boot of her car to save time next day.

Just before going to bed, she went down to see Owen. "I've packed my things, Mr. Lang. I shall leave early. I'll be gone before morning, before you're up and before –" the words caught in her throat, "before Candy wakes."

He nodded. "Thank you for all you've done, Miss Paton. In spite of – everything, it has been appreciated."

Their hands met, their eyes, too, briefly, then she went to the door. She turned. "When you marry Miss Randall, Mr. Lang, I hope you'll be very happy." She was surprised at the steadiness of her own voice. She went upstairs to bed.

But not to sleep. For most of the night, it eluded her. She tossed and turned and as the darkness gave way to a bright glow in the sky, heralding the sunrise, she got up and crept into the bathroom to wash.

She dressed, put on her coat and carried her suitcases on to the landing. Silently, holding her breath, she opened Candy's door for a last look at her. Her face, angelic in sleep, was more enchanting than ever in its relaxed, defenceless state.

"Kim," Candy whispered in her sleep.

Tears ran unchecked down Kim's cheeks. She closed the door, picked up the cases, crept past Owen's room and went down the stairs.

She put the cases down to unbolt the front door.

"Goodbye, Kim." She turned swiftly. Owen had come

from the sitting-room. He was dressed for bed, a blue patterned dressing-gown covering his pyjamas. His hands were thrust into his pockets and he looked tired beyond words.

"I tried not to wake you," Kim said.

"I haven't been asleep."

"Oh, I'm sorry."

They stared at each other and Kim could not tear her eyes away. This was like dying a little. She had to get it over. She picked up a case, raised the other hand to open the door, felt the bracelet he had given her jangling on her wrist.

She put the case down again. "I intended returning your gift by post, but since you're here, I might as well give it to you." She struggled with the catch.

"Keep it."

Her eyes jerked up at his harsh tone, but she tried again to remove the bracelet, her fingers clumsier than ever.

"I said *keep it*!"

"I can't, I mustn't, it would be wrong . . ."

His tone became urgent. "Don't sever the only link I shall have with you in the future, Kim." His voice was strained, as if he found it an effort to talk.

Her hands dropped to her sides, the bracelet hanging yellow-gold and cold over her hand. "What do you mean?" Her eyes implored him for an explanation.

"What do I mean?" His eyes looked haunted. "I mean that the thought of never seeing you again, of not having you here waiting for me when I come home, and having to spend the rest of my life without you, is driving me crazy. I mean I love you." He looked away. "I'm sorry, but I had to tell you before you left."

She whispered, unbelieving, "What did you say?"

"I said I love you."

She was bewildered. "But, Owen . . ."

"You'd better go, before Candy wakes."

"But, Owen, if you love me, why are you sending me away?"

"My darling Kim," he said softly. "I'm not sending you away. But I've got to let you go. You have your life in front of you. I wouldn't dream of expecting you to take on the burden of a husband and a ready-made family at your age, simply because I love you. You must start afresh, begin at the beginning with someone of your own choice, your own age-group. And there's your career –"

"But, Owen," the tears began again, "I don't want to go. I want to stay with you, more than anything in the world, I want to stay."

"Because of Candy?"

"Because of – you. I love you."

He moved a few paces towards her. 'Is this the truth?" His voice sounded hoarse.

"It's the truth, Owen." She moistened her lips. "I promise I'll never lie to you again as long as I live."

He opened his arms and she ran into them. They wrapped about her and his mouth found hers. He whispered, against her lips, "*Thou art my life, my love, my heart, the very eyes of me, And hast command of every part to live and die for thee.*"

She drew away a little. "So you remembered that poem?"

"Remembered it? Since I read it on that scrap of paper, I've quoted it to myself almost every time I've come within touching distance of you." He held her away and looked at her.

"Take your coat off, Kim. You've come home, my darling."

He unbuttoned it and removed it from her. It dropped to the floor and they kissed even more passionately.

He took her into the sitting-room and they shared an arm-chair. She whispered, "Hold me, Owen, hold me close so that I know this is really happening and it's not a wonderful dream."

With joy he complied with her wishes and the sun rose triumphantly into a cloudless sky. After a long, long time she stirred and smiled up at him. "What's Newton's third law of motion? I'm dying to know."

He laughed and it was gay and carefree. "Your brother's comment on your birthday card? He knows a thing or two, that brother of yours. Just wait till I met him! The first law of motion goes like this. 'If a body is at rest, it will remain at rest, and if it is in motion, it will remain in motion at a constant velocity (speed, to you) in a straight line, unless it is acted upon by a force.' The 'body in motion' was presumably me, moving through life in a straight line, disliking women. The 'force' was you, acting upon me! In other words, you knocked me sideways! But he didn't mention Newton's third law of motion, did he? 'To every action there is an equal and opposite reaction.' Every time you made it plain by what you said and did that you disliked me and all I stood for, the more I reacted by loving you and all you stood for! Tell that one to your brother, my darling."

"Berenice?" she whispered.

"Is beautiful, as beautiful as my first wife was, Kim. But, like my first wife, she's cold and hard. I could no more think of repeating my mistake by marrying her than anyone who has fallen from a cliff-top and got badly hurt could voluntarily climb back to the top of the cliff and do the same thing all over again."

She put up a hand and touched his cheek. "Thank you for telling me."

After a while, Owen said, "This job, Kim — there's no need for you to turn it down just because you're going to marry me."

She looked up at him eagerly. "You wouldn't mind if I took it on? It might involve some intensive research."

"All the better. It should help to get that excellent brain of yours into working order again. Maybe the cogs will need oiling at first, having allowed your intellect to fall into disrepair by acting as my housekeeper," he joked.

"I'm sorry, darling."

"For heaven's sake, Kim, what for?"

"For having the thing you so dislike — an arts degree."

"Dislike is too strong a word, love. It's simply that, being a scientist myself, I can't see any place for such things in the modern world."

"Anyway," she said with some satisfaction, "I only got a pass degree in English Lit., which is nothing much to be proud of."

He laughed, and for a man who had declared he had not slept he sounded surprisingly fresh. "You mean that because you aren't all that good at it, you think I should excuse you and say 'all is forgiven?'" She nodded and he kissed her thoroughly to prove beyond doubt that he had forgiven her.

"Owen?" He looked at her. "If you hadn't come back early from the conference –"

"Don't think about it, Kim. It's best forgotten. You want to know why I cut the dinner that night?" She nodded and he whispered in her ear, "You may not believe it, but I wanted to get back to you. I had been thinking of you all day and wondering what you were doing. I kept getting an odd feeling that I must get home, that you needed me. I'm not usually the type to have premonitions, but this time I did. Unscientific though they may be, I shall never laugh at such things again."

She reminded him with mischief in her eyes, "You vowed that no matter what, you wouldn't marry your housekeeper."

"And I kept my word, young woman. You dismissed yourself from my service, although – I can tell you now – I had no intention of getting rid of you. How could I when I loved you so much? Therefore, I'm not marrying my housekeeper, am I?"

"That," she smiled up at him, "sounds suspiciously like twisting the truth to suit your own purposes."

"In one word, I suppose you mean sophistry. Perhaps you're right, but in the circumstances, I think I could be forgiven, don't you?"

She nodded, her cheek rubbing against his chest. She sighed with contentment.

"In the morning," she said, snuggling closer, and as oblivious as he was to the fact that the birds in the garden were doing their best to tell the world that morning had already arrived, "in the morning we'll tell Candy."

FREE!!!!
Did you know......?

that just by mailing in the coupon below you can receive a brand new, up-to-date "Harlequin Romance Catalogue" listing literally hundreds of Harlequin Romances you probably thought were out of print.

Now you can shop in your own home for novels by your favorite Harlequin authors — the Essie Summers you wanted to read, the Violet Winspear you missed, the Mary Burchell you thought wasn't available anymore!

They're all listed in the "Harlequin Romance Catalogue". And something else too — the books are listed in numerical sequence, — so you can fill in the missing numbers in your library.

Don't delay —. mail the coupon below to us today. We'll promptly send you the "Harlequin Romance Catalogue"

FREE!